Please Stop the Music

Jim Fallon

I0567801

Acknowledgments

Copyright © 2012, 2013 James Fallon

Published by:
Storyteller Place
P.O. Box 990846
Boston, MA 02199
www.storytellerplace.com
info@storytellerplace.com

Cover by Rick Menard, copyright © 2013 James Fallon

Editing by Erica Orloff at Editing for Authors

Additional editing by Jennifer Wheet

To Mary and Mary, wherever you are, I hope you are laughing, enjoying the music, and dancing.

ONE

Kevin McCormick knew that if his father were still alive, he never would have approved of what he was about to do. He sat in the office of his funeral home, wrestling with his decision one last time. Thirty-seven years old, he still struggled with the voice of his father in his head telling him to "think about what you're doing!" He was sitting at the same desk that his father had used for decades, rocking back and forth in the same wooden, squeaky, wobbly desk chair that his father had worn out over the years. It had been four years since his father Harry died and left him alone in charge of McCormick Funeral Home.

This morning Kevin was about to fire Harry's long-time employee and best friend, the home's embalmer, Boyd Oakley. Boyd's role for nearly four decades at the home was not only as the embalmer, but also as the chief cosmetician and restorative artist. He rarely had any interaction with any of the families or friends of the deceased. Boyd had two rooms to perform his work. He alternated between them depending on the volume of corpses or the degree of their stench; if the smell from a corpse was too overwhelming, he might take a break from it and move to the other room to work on another one. Although Boyd's rooms were located in a separate wing from the viewing and gathering areas for families and friends of the deceased, they were only a few feet down the hall from the home's main offices.

Boyd had always enjoyed admonishing Kevin around the funeral home, even before Kevin's father Harry had passed. As Harry became increasingly ill during his last few years, perhaps Boyd was becoming aware that Kevin would be his boss sooner than later and began to assert his status with his sapient retorts. Kevin always respected Boyd and relied on his wisdom; the playful bantering had been a feature of their relationship since he was a teenager.

Despite their strong friendship, there was one thing that drove Kevin mad about Boyd, especially around the business: Boyd's passion for music. Boyd was an extremely avid music lover; when he wasn't listening to it, he'd often be humming, whistling, or simply tapping a tune to himself. Boyd had played trumpet in his childhood and teenage years, toyed around with drums, and learned to play a few simple melodies on the piano. He was good enough with the trumpet to play for bands in small clubs around Boston during the sixties, when some of his family moved to the area to escape the more volatile scene in Birmingham, Alabama.

Boyd had met his wife Anita while studying at Boston University, alma mater of his idol Martin Luther King Jr., and then he returned with her to Birmingham. However, at about the time that they began to settle down to raise a family, four young girls were killed in a bombing at the 16th Street Baptist Church: the final straw that convinced them to move north. They weren't entirely comfortable with Boston either, but they liked the area and thought of it as a better environment.

Boyd was a music junkie, a walking encyclopedia of many genres, especially of American blues, jazz, rock, and country. In recent years he seemed to have more trouble keeping up with the latest artists and songs, as if his musical memory bank had become oversaturated.

Harry often allowed Boyd to play his music as loudly as he wanted during work, despite Kevin's pleas for more professionalism in the workplace. Whenever Kevin complained to his father, Harry simply told him to either learn to enjoy it or buy some earplugs. His dad explained that it was a critical function of Boyd's process. Kevin never believed him and never stopped trying to convince Harry to pull the plug on the noise. He would challenge his father to name any embalming school that listed music as necessary to the process. Whenever Kevin had the chance, for example after hearing a news story about a musician being arrested or an outbreak of violence at a concert, he would remind his father that music was at the root of many problems in society.

"Some cultures don't even allow music at all," Kevin would say.

Unlike Boyd, Kevin's experiences with music had become progressively negative over the years. In grammar school he was a member of the chorus for a few months, the only boy in it. Not only did this lead to constant tormenting from the other boys, but also ridicule even from the girls in the club, telling him he sounded like a frog. "Frog" became his nickname for weeks until he quit chorus, leaving music behind for ice hockey, a sport at which he excelled and quickly ended the "sissy Frog" comments.

Eventually, however, Kevin returned to music, joining the middle school band as a trombone player. He was horrible, despite the band instructor's impeccable patience and encouragement. Like chorus, this endeavor also came to a crashing halt during his first live school performance. The band instructor, no doubt realizing that Kevin's horrible playing would destroy the recital, gave him only two or three notes for each song, telling Kevin to just master those few notes during the weeks leading up to the event.

The instructor's plan backfired, as Kevin's isolated notes actually ended up overwhelming the band's performance; after a series of bars, Kevin would interject with one of his overbearing, off-key blurts. Each time, the audience broke into laughter, regardless of how great the rest of the music sounded. At one point, between songs, a member of the audience shouted, "It sounds like a dying fart!" and everyone—including the band—roared. Kevin sat through the next few songs, intentionally not playing the instrument at all. As the curtain was drawing closed before the encore, he snuck off the stage, leaving behind the trombone as well as his musical aspirations.

As Kevin grew into adulthood, it seemed that many of his worst experiences were somehow related to music—especially pop music. As someone who thought of music as a petty, noisy, stain on society, a marketing gimmick designed to exploit the wallets of impressionable popular-culture fanatics, Kevin was perplexed and irritated with his father's tolerance for music in the funeral home. The McCormick practice even went so far as to include an odd, unique part of their planning process in which they would ask the family of the deceased about the types of music that the person had enjoyed. It was a question that always made Kevin uncomfortable to ask. It usually elicited a puzzled response, as families wondered why the funeral home cared so much about that one irrelevant detail. Since he began working at the funeral home, he always believed that one day the home's music policy would culminate in some sort of disaster involving him.

Then, after fifteen years of debate regarding the home's laissez-fare music policy, Harry died and left Kevin in charge. Kevin didn't change the music policy at first. He was too depressed initially to do much at all, and Boyd's music in a strange way reminded him fondly of the arguments it had caused with his father. Those arguments never became overly contentious; they simply ended with Kevin laughing with a comment such as, "Dad, really, you can't tell me that song isn't scraping along your spine right now?" or "Dad, are your ears bleeding yet?"

After Harry died however, Kevin spent much more time in the main offices down the hall from Boyd's music. And he became increasingly irritable and short-fused. He respected Boyd, his commitment to the home, and his relationships with his father and the other employees, but after three years of trying to tolerate the music, Kevin had frankly had enough. Everyone around the home knew that it was inevitable that the music in the embalming room was eventually going to be put to a stop. When Kevin finally decided to call Boyd into his office to break the news, Boyd didn't complain. He simply nodded and said, "I understand, Mr. McCormick." It was the first and only time that Boyd had referred to Kevin as "Mister."

Yet, for everyone including Kevin, the weeks immediately following the new "no music" rule were even more stressful than when music was allowed. It was the biggest change in the history of the home, which had been running that way in Malden, Massachusetts, a Boston suburb, for decades, since Boyd joined the firm in 1974. The other funeral home employees began to quietly glare at Kevin, treating him as if he were a dictator. The entire atmosphere shifted from one in which everyone enjoyed dealing with death into one in which Kevin felt everyone wished *he* was dead. Even his mother, Dotty, who ran the flower shop in the adjacent building, stormed into his office one day and said, "Kevin, are you out of your mind? You can't do that to Boyd!"

After the first few days, his administrative assistant, Missy Whitehead, who had worked for his father for over twenty years, threatened to quit. "You don't understand Boyd," she scolded him. "Music is his blood. And you're sucking him dry!"

She began referring to Kevin as "Count," short for "Count Dracula," and even when managing phone calls while Kevin was in the same room, she would answer, "Good morning, Count Dracula's Funeral Home, can I help you?"

The most unbearable part of the transition, however, was the shocking deterioration in Boyd's work, particularly in cosmetology. The bodies began to look horrific, one zombie-like corpse after another, and infused with a barrage of problems. People constantly complained that their deceased loved ones didn't resemble anything close to their living appearance. An unprecedented number of clients opted for a closed casket after seeing the body post-embalmment and cosmetics. During one wake, Kevin overhead a huddle of older women discussing the probable reasons why the funeral home had made the corpse look like "a ten-cent whore." At another, there was a raucous commotion when some of the children approached the casket and burst into laughter, shouting a series of jokes such as "Hey, Grampa looks like a clown!" and "Grampa's going to heaven as a transvestite!"

Kevin partially refunded several clients, but it was never enough to fully reconcile things. Whenever he asked, "What else can I do to clear this up?" the clients would reply with a variation of the same suggestion: "You should fire your cosmetician!"

Today, that suggestion was about to be enacted. Kevin was tired of hearing bickering about his no-music rule. He was relieved that he wouldn't have to ask the silly "question" any longer. Moreover, with Boyd gone, he could be more confident in the production of the embalming room.

It had been a year of rising tension in the home, not only with employees but also with clients and, even more damaging, with the local community. The reputation of McCormick Funeral Home was suffering, and the flow of corpses had slowed to a painful pace. For the first time since he began working for his father, they were operating in the red, and Kevin was unsure of how much longer it would be before McCormick Funeral Home itself was dead.

His father had many times warned him that as the manager of the home, he would have to make unpopular decisions. The "no music" policy was the first. But firing Boyd, who was loved by and close to everyone associated with the home, would be the most unpopular decision ever made. Nevertheless, he had no choice but to do just that. The decision wasn't simply about Boyd; it was about the fate of the business. His disastrous work was destroying the business and left him no choice. Kevin had prepared to leave him with a huge severance, equivalent to almost three years' pay plus continued medical coverage: an exceptional package for the mortuary field but one that Kevin hoped would settle his guilty conscience. Boyd, in his seventies, was nearing his retirement anyway…or so Kevin rationalized.

He had been secretly interviewing beauticians and embalmers, aware of the controversy that would explode by firing Boyd. He was ready to hire one of the candidates, who would work alongside another current McCormick Funeral Home employee, Dooley Hammond, Boyd's understudy for most of the past two years.

Kevin's heart began to race as he heard the familiar jingle of Boyd's keys unlock the front door of the home. He heard Boyd whistle as he strolled through the home, towards the hallway that led to Kevin's office and the embalming room. Kevin had heard the whistling hundreds of times and was genuinely heartbroken that this would be the last time.

There's no easy way to do this. But I have to be firm.

"Boyd!" Kevin called him as he walked past the office, passing from view.

The whistling stopped. Boyd was usually the first one to arrive each day, so there was no doubt he'd be surprised to realize Kevin was there. There was an odd silence that fell in the home before Boyd appeared in the doorway to the office.

"You're early," Boyd commented.

"Boyd," Kevin began as his eyes welled, "we need to talk."

"I figured we did."

"It's been going on too long."

"I know."

As Boyd's lanky body trudged into the office, retrieving his keys to the home to return them, Kevin could see that he knew what was about to happen. Nevertheless, in a strange twist, it was *Boyd* who continued the conversation by consoling *Kevin*.

"It's all right, Kevin," Boyd said in his cool, calm, alto voice, "You're all right with me. I knew this day was coming. I've heard around town that you were trying to find someone to replace me. You're a good man. I was proud to work for you and your dad. You have a very different style than your old man, but a good, strong, principled work ethic, and I understand that you think you're doing the best thing to keep this business going. You're going to be a great mortician. And I'll always have your back."

It was a serious, somber tone, very different from the playful banter and insulting that they usually exchanged. Boyd left a small package on Kevin's desk. He said, "This is for you," and shook Kevin's hand. Then he simply turned towards the door.

"Boyd, wait," Kevin said, confused and somewhat stunned.

"What else, Kevin?" Boyd hesitated in midstride.

"I have this severance pay for you. I'm not letting you leave without—"

Boyd interrupted with a single wave of his hand, smiling. "You and your dad have paid me well over the years," he said, "I couldn't ask for more. Keep it."

"Well, I wanted to offer you a part-time role, too."

"What's that?"

"As a business advisor, like an exclusive consultant to us. You've got a lot of experience. I thought that maybe you could have a part-time job here, stopping by every now and then, checking in on things."

Boyd laughed. "Son, I'm not going to charge you for my friendship. If you run into something, give me a call. I would love to chat."

Once again, Boyd steered towards the door. For Kevin—as much as he had thought and planned for it—the exchange was surreal and unexpected. As much as Boyd had tried to soften the blow, which oddly enough had seemed to land more on Kevin rather than Boyd, the young funeral home owner felt it was all wrong. He had never fired anyone prior to this.

"Boyd," Kevin called to him again.

"My God, kid," Boyd snapped, "I've made it easy for you!" He laughed, "What else?"

"There's something I've been wondering about, something I've got to ask. It's been driving me crazy these past few weeks."

"Something's been driving *you* crazy? Now that's a surprise!" Boyd joked.

"Yeah, yeah, but I've got to know. Here's the thing. What happened to you? You think it's…your age? Or…I have to admit, I thought you might be trying to get back at me about the new music ban. Were you that upset with me?"

Boyd turned completely around to face Kevin. He stepped closer, pulled up a chair, and sat. He shook his head in disbelief, glanced at the ceiling as if his dignity had been attacked, and slowly exhaled. He sat back in the chair, placing his seasoned arms and hands on the armrests, and spoke.

"Son, here's your first consultation," he began. "To some people—to most people—their work is their life. Now, *our* work is death, so it's a bit ironic that death in many ways breathes life into the people that work here, including me. I'm not sure what's going to happen to me now because I'm addicted to this work. It *is* my life. My job is to revive these bodies to a state that reflects who they were, what they were all about. And to give people one final, absolute, glimpse of their loved ones.

"In order to do that, I need a channel to connect to them. Pictures and stories only take you so far. A lot of pictures are too carefully posed, and most stories are full of bull. I need to relate to their soul.

"Now, you don't like music, so this is the part you won't understand, but I'll say it anyway: music is the medium that allows me to connect to these people. I feel music. It runs through my veins, my heart, my mind...my soul. For sure. I've got to have the music in order to function, in order to do my job, in order to reach into these people's lives. It's the way I've been doing this job for about fifty years, before you were born.

"I would never sabotage your business, although, yes, I was a bit angry at you at first for changing your dad's policy. And don't *ever* imply that I'm too old.

"But here is the lesson: when you take away someone's tools, you cannot expect them to get the job done. My most essential tool...is...*music*."

Kevin still didn't grasp this desperate necessity. He was sure that Boyd was in denial about his age; Boyd just didn't have the touch any more. But the new employee was not expected to start yet, so he decided to give Boyd one more chance to prove him wrong.

"Okay Boyd," he sternly replied, "What if I were to reverse the policy? Maybe not completely, but revise it a bit?"

"You're giving me my music back?"

"Yes, but you have to keep the door closed to the embalming room, and if I hear it, you lose it."

Boyd grinned. "I'm glad you understand!"

Kevin returned a blank stare.

"You still don't understand, do you?" Boyd asked.

"No. No, Boyd, I don't. But I'm giving you probation, for one week. We had some calls that I haven't answered yet because I wasn't sure when the new people could start. But I'll call those clients back, and tell them we can handle their arrangements. I'm serious Boyd: if things don't change this week, I'm sorry but I'll have to let you go. No excuses. None. I don't care what condition they're in when they get here. There is a business at stake here. I am putting my foot down. I hate to do it, but there are a lot of people who need this business to keep running."

"Don't worry. I won't let you down. I promise."

Boyd stood, retrieved the small package from Kevin's desk, and started out of the room.

"What was in that package?" Kevin asked.

"That, my friend," Boyd announced as he walked out the door, "is for the day when we *do* part ways. Not today!"

TWO

The first corpse to arrive during Boyd's probationary period was that of a young woman, twenty-five years old, named Britney Kerrigan. Britney had driven her car at eighty miles an hour into a block of trees. She was not wearing a seatbelt and was driving under the influence of drugs. Parts of the car broke free as it burst into sections through the trees and continued to tumble down a rocky hill. Although firefighters were able to recover nearly the entire vehicle, they couldn't locate all of her body parts. Her mangled face was barely recognizable; her distraught mother had to identify her based on a neck tattoo and a birthmark on her back.

When the *first* round of her disassembled body parts arrived at the funeral home, Kevin realized that the ultimatum he had placed on Boyd was unfair: there was no way anyone could put her back together. The parents simply requested that McCormick Funeral Home do their best, but they were content to have a closed-casket wake given the circumstances.

About an hour after the first round arrived, the fire department called to let the home know that they had returned to the crash site and located some more body parts.

Dooley Hammond, Kevin's best friend, who had been working at the home since only a few years after Kevin himself, took the call. Dooley had a special history with Boyd and the home, and for that reason Kevin was well aware that Dooley was the only other employee who would take Boyd's firing harder than himself.

Kevin had known Dooley since their days at St. Paul's Prep School. In those days Dooley was somewhat of an outcast, caught up in the post-punk rock scene of the 1980s, attracted to bands like Echo and the Bunnymen, The Clash, the Sex Pistols, The Psychedelic Furs, and U2 in their younger, punkier days. He and Kevin had met in detention hall one afternoon. Father Murray walked into the room full of about twenty teenagers serving various disciplinary sentences. Father was desperate because the event company that usually set up the gym and cafeteria for Bingo had not yet arrived. He offered the entire group of detainees the option to set up tables, chairs, barrels, audio equipment, and whatever else was necessary, instead of sitting in the room in silence for three hours. No one budged at first, as the students were unanimously content to stare off into space daydreaming for the afternoon, but when Father offered twenty-five dollars to anyone who would help, Kevin, Dooley, and two others jumped.

From that point, the four boys replaced the event company on Tuesdays and Saturdays. Kevin liked to work in peace, but Dooley would blast his music all afternoon. It was the punk music in particular that made Kevin's stomach churn; it reminded him of an incident that occurred during his freshman year. Kevin was one of the smaller students whose growth spurt arrived a little late, subjecting him to crosschecks in the high school hallways and the occasional shove into an empty locker of the male-only prep school. One afternoon, to avoid the gauntlet of abuse that usually awaited him on his way to the bus stop, he decided to take a longer detour, out the back door of the building, around a baseball field, and to a public bus stop. His plan at first appeared perfect, as nearly all of the kids congregated towards the front of the main building, and the back door led to the faculty parking lot.

Relieved, he strolled through the lot and around the baseball field, where there was a handful of a few older students listening to "Rebel Yell" by the British punk rock singer Billy Idol. Ecstatic that his plan had worked, he nodded towards the group.

Their response was nothing short of a mood breaker.

"What are you looking at?" the tallest of them said.

"Don't you know this is our turf, you puke?" another, heavyset boy shouted.

Before Kevin could run, all six of them had surrounded him, tackled him to the ground, stolen the four dollars from his pocket, torn up his textbooks, and tossed him into a dumpster between the baseball field and the parking lot. During the whole ordeal, they shouted lyrics from the song...which had nothing to do with beating up a tiny freshman, but for some reason must have given them some sense that they were being "rebel" bad-asses. As he lay in the dumpster, pretending to be dead, he could hear their laughter, along with the sounds of Billy Idol, waning as the bullies disappeared. Kevin lay in the foul, steel enclosure—with probably a couple of city rats digging around below in the mounds of trash—cursing the music industry for promoting an image that compelled the young teenagers to torment a helpless, harmless kid.

Dooley wasn't one of those kids, but his punk music during Bingo setup reminded Kevin of that ordeal, forcing him to re-live the trauma, over and over again. Kevin complained repeatedly, until after one heated altercation he yanked the chain dangling from Dooley's left ear. From that point on, Dooley decided to wear headphones instead.

Over the years, Dooley's taste in music turned towards darker metal such as Alice Cooper, Marilyn Manson, and Black Sabbath. These were artists that had offended Harry but intrigued Boyd. Kevin couldn't and wouldn't listen to any of it. Dooley was one of the kindest, most understanding people Kevin had ever met: a stark contrast from the popular perception of the music to which he was drawn.

Despite doing well in high school, Dooley struggled in college, dropping out and bouncing from one job to the next. He had been fired several times. The reasons, he would explain to Kevin, were usually because of his appearance and musical preference. In those years–in his twenties—Dooley abandoned his purple-spiked-hair from high school, but he still often wore rings through his lips, nose, or eyebrows and always wore his long dark hair in a disheveled arrangement that made Kevin wonder if he woke up that way.

Having an interest in cosmetics, Dooley had tried his hand in beauty salons for a while, even taking courses in cosmetology and hair design. This was a passion of his since his days as a punk-rocker, and it evolved as glam-metal bands like Poison, Van Halen, and Twisted Sister exploded onto the rock scene. However, one after another, beauty salons also fired him, blaming his appearance and style for scaring away customers. He would too often try to convince clients to take a walk on the wilder side with their makeovers.

When Kevin—who had completed a mortician program and received his funeral director's license—first approached his father about hiring Dooley, Harry was reluctant. His reasons were that he never liked Dooley all that much because of his appearance and his fascination for "disgusting, violent, bloody stuff. There is no place for someone like that in this business."

But Boyd had bonded with Dooley, as Dooley would often come around the funeral home looking for Kevin. Boyd and Dooley would occasionally take a few minutes to discuss music. Boyd increasingly looked forward to those conversations and would sometimes ask Kevin about Dooley if a stretch had passed when Dooley hadn't been by the home. Kevin pleaded to Boyd to talk to his father about hiring him. Boyd encouraged Harry to do just that, explaining that Harry had judged the kid all wrong. "He's drawn to music about rebellion, oppression, vices. It's very important to him."

"It's music about nonsense," Harry would argue, remaining skeptical. He would dismiss Boyd's recommendations with retorts such as, "Have you seen the way that Manson kid dresses?" and "I can't hire someone who idolizes a drug-addicted freak who bites the heads off of bats."

Boyd never gave up, relentlessly praising Dooley: "He has a wonderful ideology, great character."

Eventually, Harry agreed to give Dooley a shot, as long as he agreed not to wear any jewelry around work. Not only did Dooley embrace his new opportunity, but his work ethic was such that when Harry criticized Kevin for slacking or making mistakes, he often concluded by saying, "Why can't you be more like Dooley?" Harry grew to become very fond of his new employee, and in time described him as "one of the hardest-working and talented people" he'd ever known.

It was Dooley who had taken the call from the fire department that day about Britney Kerrigan's additional body parts being located. Dooley was also the only funeral home employee who knew of Kevin's plans to fire Boyd. Although he understood, he had expressed his conflicting emotions about it to Kevin. On the one hand, he liked Boyd, had immense respect for him, and without the older man's help he would probably still be washing dishes, picking up garbage, or even unemployed. On the other hand, he agreed that Boyd's work had been absurdly awful for months. Dooley had been occasionally working alongside Boyd for a few years, assisting him in both embalming and cosmetology, so he had witnessed it firsthand and often found himself trying to correct Boyd's mistakes. The constant stress had even impeded the development of Dooley's own talent as a cosmetician.

Dooley was distraught when he broke the news about Kerrigan to Kevin, "Dude, this is all wrong," he told

Kevin, "Even the best of the best could not put this girl back together. I mean, her body is coming in here in pieces, literally, waves of pieces, Kev. You going to give this guy an impossible job and then fire him because he didn't execute? That's just…being a complete asshole."

Dooley was right. Accepting this, Kevin went to the embalming room to deliver the message to Boyd about more of Britney being on the way. He was prepared to temporarily call off the ultimatum.

As he entered the room, Boyd was staring sullenly over the woman's body parts. Kevin handed Boyd a few pictures of Britney that the family had given him to help try to assemble her into something that resembled her living appearance.

"Boyd, listen, I know what I said, but I'm going to overlook this one."

Boyd raised his arm as if to silence him. "We had a deal," he insisted, "I made a promise. And besides, this girl did not deserve this. Did you ask the question?"

"The what?"

"The question. About what type of music she listened to?"

"Oh, yeah, yeah," Kevin replied, rifling through papers on the clipboard of the woman's funeral arrangements. "Umm, here it is," he read the paper as he handed it to Boyd, "Apparently she was a big Amy Winehouse fan. And Macy Gray, Sarah Vaughan."

The tension on Boyd's face grew. He already had what appeared to be an insurmountable task at hand, but on top of that Kevin's reply was not what he expected. "Amy who?" he said, exasperated as he read the paper. He read the name closely, then began to scroll through his computer's endless library of music trying to find it.

"Never heard of her," he said as he came across her biggest hit, "Rehab."

In contemplative desperation, Boyd stared into Kevin's face as he listened to the first few verses, which described someone with a substance abuse problem who refused to go to a rehabilitation clinic.

Like most songs, Kevin hated that one too. "You know," he said, "I think she also died of drugs or alcohol abuse or something."

When Kevin left the embalming room, he was sure that he was going to have to fire Boyd—again—based on their agreement and Boyd's insistence to honor it. It was not the way he wanted their working relationship to end. He was disappointed that Boyd would not get a real chance to prove that it was the absence of music that was destroying his capability.

Kevin lay awake throughout that night, realizing he'd made an unrealistic demand that was going to cost Boyd his livelihood. More unsettling was that this type of ultimatum was certainly not a business tactic his father would have condoned.

The next morning, when Kevin arrived at the home, Boyd was already there. He could hear Boyd's music playing despite the door being closed to the embalming room. Kevin approached the room, once again prepared to withdraw the ultimatum, at least for this body. However, when he opened the door, he was surprised to see Boyd smiling and humming along to the blaring music as he put the finishing touches of make-up on Britney's face.

"Did you know Winehouse was a Sam Cooke fan?" Boyd grinned, "And she liked Lesley Gore, too!"

"Really?" After years of working with this man so addicted to music, Kevin knew that Cooke was one of Boyd's favorite musicians.

"You know, Sam Cooke? She did a cover of 'Cupid,' one of his hits. Such a great song." He sang the first few lines for Kevin.

"Never heard it."

"Too bad. You know, it's strange: he's another one that died before his time. Shot in a hotel when he was thirty-three. A raw, soulful sound. I know you've heard me play his stuff many times."

"I know, probably, but I try to block it out," Kevin said as he walked closer to the embalming table.

"That's a shame. This Winehouse was a shame, too. So talented. Like someone snatched her out of the Supremes, sprinkled some Mick Jagger onto her, and sent her through a time machine forty years forward." He stepped back from the woman's body on the table.

"Well, what do you think?"

Kevin approached the body. In one of the rarest occasions since he had been working at the home, he was shocked. He thought he knew of Boyd's capabilities, but after the disasters in previous months, he was certain before he walked into that room that Boyd's career was finished. He had wondered all night if the young woman's fate in the car was meant to collide with Boyd's in the funeral business. It seemed almost fitting that there would be a Sam Cooke connection as he worked on his final body.

However, standing over Britney, Kevin was speechless. The woman's finished appearance was Boyd's masterpiece. There wasn't even a trace of the mangled mess that had come into the home. Rather, her face was so lifelike that Kevin could not believe she was actually dead. He could feel her personality glowing from her body, just as her family had described it: her relentlessly charming wit. The corners of her mouth just barely hinted of the smiles in the pictures from her family, reflecting her fun-loving nature. Her ever-so-slightly raised eyebrows left a trace of her garrulousness. The angle of her chin, the semi-organized tousled curls in her hair, the makeup somehow emanating a lively glow from her cheeks, jaw, and eyelids—all captured her personality.

He felt her soul.

"She was a beautiful girl," Boyd noted. "Gone too soon, much too soon. Well?"

Kevin uttered, "I…I…I think…"

"You think what?"

"I think they'll be having an open-casket ceremony."

THREE

Three weeks passed since the Britney Kerrigan incident. As he promised, Kevin reversed his "no music" policy and had been allowing Boyd to play it ever since. There were no more questions about whether Boyd had lost his touch: each corpse since had been revitalized to perfection. Kevin was aware that whenever he was outside the office, Boyd would open the door to the embalming room and blast the music throughout the home, as long as there wasn't a viewing service in progress. The rest of the staff didn't seem to mind, and Kevin believed they actually enjoyed it. Occasionally, when Kevin was in the office, he would have to go down the hall, knock on the door, and ask Boyd to lower the volume. Otherwise he was learning to tolerate the noise.

However, Boyd's superior work wasn't enough to prevent the slowing flow of business. Momentarily starved for dead bodies, Kevin was taking advantage of anyone who was dead or even thinking about dying, including one of this morning's prospects: Esther Best, an elderly woman who had called the home yesterday and arranged to meet him personally at Malden Hospital. Kevin parked his car, an old Cadillac that once belonged to his dad, in the hospital lot, preparing to meet this unique client. Esther, of whom Kevin had never heard, also claimed to have "at one time belonged to" his father.

Dignified and articulate, she was on her deathbed at the hospital. She had told Kevin to meet her there "the sooner the better." As Kevin approached her room, he realized that he had never been less comfortable meeting a client. He wondered if his mother knew about Esther, and whether she would approve of him accepting her as a client. He was curious about the nature of his father's "connection" with Esther, although he was trying hard not to think about the circumstances that led to their "arrangement."

Inside the room, Kevin was greeted by a loud, mucous-filled discharge from Esther's neighbor, whose bed was closest to the door. The curtain between the woman and Esther was drawn almost completely.

"Mrs. Best?" Kevin called.

"Who is it?" a young, healthy woman's voice from behind the curtain asked.

"Kevin McCormick, McCormick Funeral Home," Kevin replied, delighted to hear the sound of a healthy voice.

"Come here, dear," another ailing female voice gasped.

Kevin passed through the curtain. There was Esther, just as she had described, plugged with countless tubes. Kevin had been in this situation before—helping someone arrange their funeral from his or her deathbed—but this time it was difficult for him not to stare at the machines that were helping her get through the hour.

"Hi," he said softly, placing his hand on her bandaged hand, bruised most likely from numerous repositioning of intravenous tubes. Esther took her other hand and clasped it around his.

"Mrs. Best, I'm Kevin."

She grinned as widely as her ailing face would allow and said, "You look just like your father."

Something about the way she delivered it made Kevin cringe. He withdrew his hand.

"Call me 'Etty,' handsome," Esther said, staring into his eyes.

Kevin's discomfort induced him to try and deflect the direction of Esther's misguided advances. He turned to the other woman in the room. She was sitting in a chair next to the bed, amused as if she was trying to control her laughter. Kevin guessed she was in her thirties.

"Hi. Kevin," he introduced himself, reaching to shake her hand.

She leaned forward, gingerly took his hand, and introduced herself, "Amy Best. Etty's daughter."

Her greeting was interrupted by another jarring, loud, mucous-laden roar from the woman in the next bed.

"I'm sorry you have to share a room with *The Exorcist*," Kevin joked.

Amy laughed.

"The what?" Esther asked, confused.

"Never mind, Mom, it was just a joke," Amy said, pointing to the woman behind the curtain.

"Oh, and a sense of humor, too," Esther said, staring at Kevin. "You know, Amy, these McCormicks have good genes."

"Mom, please!"

"Well, Mr. McCormick," Esther sighed, "here it is. Some are more prepared for it than others, but I don't think anyone ever is fully prepared, you know? You don't know quite where you'll be…when you expire. Or who will be with you. For me, as prepared as I was, I never imagined I'd be enjoying my final few days on earth in the luxury of this hospital—*wheeze*—in the comfort of blinking lights and beeps and a number of tubes inserted into my body—*pause, wheeze*—while enjoying the sounds of phlegm-filled cough of the woman with whom I share this room. *Soft, barely audible, muffled cough.* She has emphysema."

Then she raised her voice, as if to announce to her hospital roommate, "And she might be dead before I am!"

Her roommate returned Esther's prediction with a forced, phlegm-filled cough.

"Yes," Esther wheezed, "I knew your father…very well. I was Harry's lover before he married your mother." The tone of her voice assumed an impish quality, as if she expected Kevin to be surprised and perhaps even unnerved by her revelation.

She lowered her voice and continued. "When your father and I were together—well, we were never *together* really—when your father and I were *enjoying* each other's company, he assured me that when my time was up, McCormick Funeral Home would send me off 'in style' were his exact words.

"Now, Mr. McCormick, I'm sure your father never told you about me. We were never in love. We were just two ships passing in the night. Well, more like two sex-craving yachts sharing the harbor for a while. But we shared a connection. And I would only trust your home with my funeral. I hope you will respect the friendship and arrangement that your father and I had."

Kevin was intrigued, but wasn't sure how much more he wanted to hear about his father's casual-romantic exploits.

"Certainly," he interrupted, attempting to derail her train of thought, "Absolutely. McCormick Funeral Home will honor any requests you had made in the past with my father. And you can call me 'Kevin' by the way."

"Oh, really? Are you hitting on me, young McCormick?"

Kevin wasn't sure how she was drawing that conclusion. "No, no, no, absolutely not. I ask all of our customers to call me 'Kevin.'"

"That's unfortunate. That would have been a nice way to go out."

"Mom, please," Amy shouted with an amused grin.

"No, really, Amy," Esther continued, pointing to Kevin's crotch, "If he's anything like his father, and it appears that he is…"

"Mom," Amy interrupted, lifting herself from the chair enough that she could seize Esther's hands to prevent them from gesturing towards Kevin's groin. With ease, Amy wrestled the weakening woman's hands back towards her stomach.

The effort to converse had winded Esther, and it took her a moment to catch her breath. She rested comfortably back into the bed, gazing up into space, before gaining enough strength to speak, "Are you single, Kevin?"

He knew this was going in an entirely unprofessional direction, so once again he attempted to steer the conversation back to its intended course.

"Mrs. Best, we really have to talk about your arrangements."

She lifted her head slightly so that she could glare at him, "You're asking me to care about a party that I'm not going to attend?"

"No, no, hardly. I mean, yes, it's your party. No, I mean, it's your funeral. I'm sorry, that all came out the wrong way." Never before had he been so nervous in meeting a client.

Esther laughed, waving to Amy for the oxygen mask. Amy held the mask over her mother's mouth for a moment. She offered Kevin an unsettled smile that told of her appreciation of Esther's sense of humor, while nervously anticipating her mother's loss. She fixed her eyes lovingly onto her mother's face as her smile dissolved into a tangled twist of warmth and anxiety. She caressed her mother's thin, white hair until Esther motioned for her to remove the mask.

"He's single, Amy. If he wasn't, he would have said so. And you're not getting any younger." She turned to Kevin, while pointing at Amy, "This girl is an angel. And at thirty-six, hasn't lost any of her looks. Isn't she beautiful?"

"Mom! Please!"

She is beautiful, Kevin thought, and with the eyes and tenderness of an angel, no doubt. Her short, blond hair was pulled back from her face, which had barely a trace of makeup. She was dressed in a simple green top, sort of a fleece-sweater thing, and jeans. She didn't appear to have put much thought into her hasty appearance. Obviously in these hours she was most concerned about her mom. Kevin figured that Amy had probably spent much if not all of her spare time, and then some, in the hospital to be with her mother during her final days. It showed in her weathered eyes. And yet, he thought, she was still gorgeous.

Thirty-six? Are you kidding me?

But he had several other clients to manage that afternoon, and this particular one was already setting his schedule back. Besides, despite what Esther was thinking, Kevin knew that a woman as beautiful as Amy would never go for a stout, balding, middle-aged funeral home mortician. The "mortician" part alone was usually enough to send the single women running away. Regardless of the setting—blind dates, double-dates, online dating chat rooms, speed dates, online dating websites—his conversations with available women almost always went along the same track:

"Oh, so what do you do for a living?"

"I'm a mortician."

"Isn't that with dead people, and bodies and funerals and stuff?"

"Yes, pretty much, yes."

"Okay, bye-bye!"

His was a profession that wasn't exactly among the most desirable for younger women, whose preferences on the dating websites were painfully predictable: doctor, athlete, lawyer, senator, money manager, at least six feet, six inches tall, no more than one hundred ninety pounds. Never once did he see any single women seeking a gently-overweight licensed funeral director.

For those women who didn't appear to care as much about a specific profession, there was often a simmering distaste for his work that was bound to explode into a fit of disgust at some point. For example, he once dated a woman who was fine with his occupation as long as he never mentioned it. One night, however, they went out for a casual evening with friends at a music-free takeout pizza joint. At the time, Kevin had a habit of pouring ketchup onto everything, from chicken to French fries to garlic bread. As the group sat at the picnic tables outside the place, Kevin began to empty ketchup packets onto slices of his favorite pizza: hamburger.

His date shot to her feet and shouted, "Okay, I can't take it anymore!"

Everyone else at the table froze.

"What is it?" Kevin asked.

"How can you do *that*," she said, pointing at his pizza, "after you've been working on dead bodies all day?!"

"What? It's just like a cheeseburger," Kevin said, trying to calm her, "Just a slightly different layout."

"You're a sick person!" she declared and stormed off, never to be seen or heard from again.

For the girlfriends who *were* willing to overlook the mortician feature, as well as his physical shortcomings, Kevin's mild hatred for music would eventually be the deal-breaker. In Kevin's eyes, however, there was bound to be someone out there who was fascinated with death and didn't like music. She would be well worth the wait.

But Esther had an agenda. That was clear. Hopeless as it was, Kevin thought that maybe if he just humored the woman a bit, things would move on quicker and he could do his job.

"Yes," he acknowledged, "You have a very beautiful daughter."

"See?!" Esther wheezed to Amy, "What's wrong with him?"

"Lots of things, Mrs. Best, lots of things," Kevin answered, "You don't even want to know."

"For instance?"

"Well, sorry to be so blunt, but death. My job is death. And most people, especially younger attractive people, don't want to be around people whose lives revolve around death. I'm sorry, I'm not trying to offend or antagonize you, but that's just the way it is Mrs. Best. So please, if we can just talk about your arrangements..."

Esther sighed, surrendering her intentions, and waved to her daughter, "Amy, that packet over there."

Amy retrieved an old, worn, manila envelope that had a McCormick Funeral Home logo, one which Kevin had never seen, stamped on the front. She handed it to Kevin.

"Your father made my arrangements before you were born," the old woman explained.

In disbelief, Kevin unbound the string that held the package closed. He removed its contents. He was struck with pleasant astonishment when he discerned that these were forms that his father had used over forty years ago, detailing everything from flowers to psalms to the cemetery plot to the style of casket to the inscription for the headstone. It was his father's writing, for sure, and everything was dated from the 1960s.

"This is," he began in shock, "this is just..."

"Vintage?" Esther finished his thought. "You can say it. But I'm not as old as I look: I'm only seventy-four. Living the good life caught up with me too quickly, but I don't regret it. I probably could have lasted another ten years if I had quit smoking and drinking earlier, and slowed down at a younger age, but then you're not 'living' as far as I'm concerned. Know what I mean?

"At any rate, everything that's in there you will still be able to get today. I hope your mother will be okay with the bouquets."

"My mother?"

"Yes, I never knew Dotty. I knew *of* her, but never met her. Your father only told me that he'd fallen for someone, and that was it. It was inevitable with us. We

32

were not in love. With Harry and me, it was just about sex, lots of *hungry* sex. You know what I'm talking about, dear? That real, hungry…"

"Okay, Mom!" Amy interrupted, jumping from her seat. She raced around the bed, grabbed a hold of Kevin's arm, and led him out of the room.

As they passed through the doorway, Kevin could hear Esther trying to shout, "You kids today! You need to get out and enjoy life!"

Amy led Kevin around the corner, where Esther couldn't hear them.

"I'm sorry about my mother," she began with a smile hinting of embarrassment.

"No, no, don't apologize, please. Your mother is quite the woman. Strong sense of humor."

She laughed. "I know. Sometimes she just doesn't have a filter though."

"I understand."

She pointed to the packet, "It should all be there. I went over all of it with her yesterday. It's amazing that even all those years ago, she knew what she'd want." She covered her mouth with one hand as her eyes welled up.

"I'm sorry, I'm so sorry," Kevin tried to console her, "We'll take care of your mother. We'll make sure she gets everything she wants in here."

She took a step towards him, gave him a light embrace, and pressed her forehead against his shoulder. It wasn't an unusual interaction: many times family members needed consolation during funeral arrangements. As a funeral home director, Kevin had to maintain a balance of professionalism. He wasn't supposed to share the grief. He also felt that it was a little disrespectful to convey in any way that he thought he understood the nature of someone else's relationship and the extent of their sorrow. However, since his father's death, he had become much more willing to offer comfort to those who appeared to need it. He softly held Amy with one arm, resting his hand on her back.

"I'm very sorry."

"Thank you, thanks," she said, pulling herself away as she wiped her tears and regained her composure. "If there's anything missing, just let me know. My number's right in there."

As she said "anything missing," it struck Kevin that, despite how thorough his father had been, even so long ago, something might be missing after all. "Well," he replied, "While I have you here, I don't recall seeing…the first time I flipped through this…I looked at it so quickly."

He examined the papers as she dabbed her eyes with a tissue.

"This must have been before…," he continued, "Well, Boyd didn't start working for my dad until the seventies, so…"

"Who? Before what?"

"Never mind," he answered, satisfied that he wasn't going to find what he was looking for in the stack of papers. He carefully returned them to the envelope and retrieved a smartphone from his pocket. "I need to know what type of music your mother likes."

Amy stood, puzzled, as all of the customers did for that question.

"Yeah, I know, it might seem like a weird question, but I've got to know, for the embalmer—the cosmetician."

She seemed even more baffled.

"I know, but it's something that helps him. It's a long story. Do you know, or can I just go back in there and ask her?"

"No, I know. She likes that big band stuff, and she used to watch those old shows like Ed Sullivan and Lawrence Welk. Big Lawrence Welk fan."

"Any particular songs? Musicians?"

"Oh, God, I don't know. Maybe you should probably just ask her while you're here."

She led him back into the room.

"Back so soon?" Esther asked, disappointed. "I was hoping you two had gone for coffee or something."

"I'm sorry Mrs. Best, but apparently there *is* something missing."

"What is it, dear?"

"We need to know if you have any favorite music, songs, or musicians."

Esther sat staring at Kevin as she tried to make sense of the query.

He stood, patiently waiting to type the information into his smartphone. "Amy was saying Lawrence Welk?"

"What?!" Esther retorted. "Are you serious? 'Lawrence Welk,' Amy?!"

"Yeah, Mom. You used to watch that show all the time?"

"Oh God, no, no, no! I only watched that because *you* liked it."

Kevin's eyebrows rose in astonishment. His attention shifted to Amy, "You like 'The Lawrence Welk Show'?"

"No! No!" Amy denied. "She tortured me with that show, for years! *You* thought *I* liked it?"

"Well, yes, honey, I did. You sat and watched it with me from start to finish hundreds of times, remember?"

"Yes, but that's because I thought *you* liked it!"

"Well, I'm sorry, honey. I never knew. You should have said something. The songs aren't bad, but those people, and that show, it's all too uptight. Too stiff for me."

"Okay," Kevin stepped in to temper the heated revelation, "Look, it's okay to like the show. The music is…was…very popular, in its day. I'm not a big fan of that music myself, but lots of people like it. Lots of nice people on that show. Nothing to be embarrassed about.

"So, Mrs. Best, please, then, what do you like?" He bobbed his head as if trying to coax her response, "Is there a sound, or an artist, that you relate to?"

"Of course, Kevin. I love music. I've got a long list of favorites. But the ones that I really *relate* to, as you put it, I would say are in a certain class to themselves. I guess you might call them 'songbirds of jazz': Ella Fitzgerald, Billie Holiday, Alicia Keys, Nora Jones, Diana Krall, Melody Gardot. There's something about those voices: the way they can just dance across those jazz scales with ease, the way they seem to share a part of themselves with every verse. 'Summertime': there's so much melancholy there for me, especially now.

"You know, there's a song I've heard a thousand times, by a thousand different people, in a thousand different places: 'Somewhere Over the Rainbow.' Never really cared for it. But Gardot does it so magnificently."

She slowly sighed, closed her eyes, and rested into her pillow in complete peace, as if she was playing the song in her mind, her cheeks swollen with a broad smile.

"Okay, Mrs. Best, I've got it. Thank you very much. It was a pleasure to meet you."

She didn't respond, instead simply laying with her eyes closed, slowly rocking her head back and forth, humming the notes in her mind. Kevin looked towards Amy.

"It's okay," she whispered. "I think she's falling asleep."

Kevin nodded and pointed to the door, letting Amy know that he was leaving.

She held up a finger to halt him for a moment, indicating that she had something to tell him first.

"Sure," he whispered, "What else can I do?"

"Oh, nothing. I just wanted to let you know that it doesn't bother me that you're a mortician. I think it takes a rare blend of person to do what you do. You have to be very strong and sensitive. I admire you and appreciate what you do. I mean it. That's all."

She smiled and waved goodbye. Kevin reciprocated the gesture and headed out of the room.

As he reached the door, he heard Esther call to him once more, "Kevin, her number is in the package!"

*   *   *

When Kevin drove out of the hospital parking lot, his head wrangled with a hurricane of emotions from that morning's meeting with Esther. He wondered if his mother knew about Harry's relationship with her, and how she'd take it. He wondered about his father's younger days and why his dad never told him about some of his wilder history. He missed his father, so it was odd but nice to meet someone who was connected to his past. And the papers, the logo, the envelope: they hadn't done business that way in years.

That was even before Boyd came along!

The white Cadillac he was driving had been his father's for almost twenty years, since Kevin was in high school. It had been painted since, but the black leather interior had all of the wear and tear from years of Harry's use. Inside it, Kevin felt close to him, as if his dad was right there in the front passenger's seat. He thought of his father in his early days at the home, how different the world was then. Around town, even after Harrys' death, strangers would still often recognize the car and acknowledge Kevin as Harry's son. They would approach Kevin and tell him stories, such as how his father handled a relative's death or how he reached out to help them during times of hardship. He admired his father's ability to repeatedly make positive impressions on people's lives: leaving a legacy of selfless influence that people like Esther and Boyd recalled with genuine appreciation.

Yet he also wondered if Esther's wake and funeral might spring more skeletons from Harry's closet.

On top of it all, there was Amy.

What a stunning woman. What was that she said, "It doesn't bother me that you're a mortician"?

Trying to get a grip on the freight train of thoughts and emotions, Kevin slowed the Cadillac down a bit as he closed his eyes and covered them with one hand. It was something he would never do, in fact, no one in their right mind driving a car at forty miles an hour would dare to do, but Kevin felt that he needed to do it, just for a tiny split-second. After all, there were no other cars around him on this wooded section along the Lynn Fells Parkway into the neighboring town of Melrose. He hadn't seen a car for a few minutes, and, knowing the road as well as he did, he was sure that there wouldn't be another one for at least a few more seconds.

Or so he thought.

When he uncovered his eyes, he was in the opposite lane, seconds from colliding into a pickup truck head-on. His only reaction was to yank the steering wheel to the right, veering it back into its proper lane.

The problem was that the truck did the same thing.

Kevin jerked the steering wheel a second time, harder, catapulting the Cadillac off into the woods, perpendicular to the direction of the road. There was no guardrail to break the momentum of the careening vehicle. His last thought before he blacked into unconsciousness was of young Britney Kerrigan.

FOUR

When Kevin awoke, he was in a hospital bed. Other than some bumps and bruises and a couple of deep gashes, he was okay. The worst of it was a huge, swollen, black and blue pillow forming on his forehead. The nurse told him that they had run a CT scan, and everything looked fine. She said he was lucky he was in an old Cadillac, "They don't make sedans that big and heavy anymore."

She said that the doctors had given him some painkillers and wanted to keep him for observation for signs of a concussion, but otherwise there was no reason he wouldn't be released later that evening.

Kevin was utterly speechless.

"Your mother will be here in a few hours to take you home," the nurse informed him. "A man named Boyd from your funeral business picked up all of your belongings from the garage that towed your car. He left you this note."

She handed it to him. It read:

Kev,

Quite a "turn" of events for you today. Sorry about the Caddy. After what you've put it through, there's nothing even I could do to make it look like anything it used to. Will need a closed casket for that one. But seriously, glad you are okay. Take a couple days off— we've got this covered at the home. Get well!— B

"So my car is totaled?" Kevin asked the nurse.

"Yes, demolished," she answered.

"Ohh, but that was my Dad's car, for over twenty years."

"Sounds like it was time for a new car."

"What happened to the pickup?"

"The driver of the pickup truck? Nothing. He pulled over and called 9-1-1. He said you kept going on and on about an 'Amy' before you completely collapsed."

"Really?"

"Yes. We've all been trying to figure out who she is. Your mother, your friend Boyd, the other people you work with: nobody's ever heard of Amy. We thought you might be delirious."

"Oh, she's just a client. Well, her mother's the client. Right before the accident, I left this hospital after meeting them."

A doctor visited him briefly to explain the symptoms of a concussion. The nurse returned and spoke to Kevin about his gashes, how they were treated, and about the medication that the doctors had prescribed for him. Other than a little pain and soreness, he felt fine, and repeated that to the nurse every twenty minutes for two hours until his mother arrived. Then he repeated that every twenty minutes until he was released another three hours later.

During the three hours that his mother sat with him in the hospital, Kevin never mentioned Esther Best, although his mother asked him at least once every twenty minutes, "Who's Amy?"

*   *   *

Kevin did stay home from work the next day, but a heartbroken voicemail from Amy Best sent him back to the home two days later.

"Mr. McCormick, this is Amy Best." Amy's voice was shattered as she sobbed, "You met my mother Etty and me earlier this week at the hospital. Etty's passed. We'd like to have her wake and funeral later this week. Please call me."

Kevin was having a hard time resting with all the pain, and he didn't like to be away from work, but above all he wanted to make sure that Harry's promise to Esther would be fulfilled. When he arrived at the home, he was surprised to hear from Missy the administrative assistant that she, Boyd, Dooley, and even Kevin's mother had all already spoken to Amy Best about the arrangements. The rest of the staff was hard at work on Esther's services, along with the other four new clients for whom Kevin had been working. Esther's wake was scheduled for Saturday, and the funeral for Sunday.

"So, my mother's doing the flowers?" Kevin asked, impressed and stunned.

"Yes," Missy answered knowingly.

Kevin paused for a moment, watching Missy work on her computer. She appeared to be aware of his stare but simply kept typing.

"Yes, your mom knew about her," she noted as she typed, "She's okay with it. Don't worry. The flowers will be beautiful."

"Has her body arrived yet?"

"Yes, earlier this morning. Boyd's been working on her. He's been waiting for the music list. It wasn't in the services packet."

"I know. My dad didn't ask for it back in those days, so I had to key it all into my smartphone," Kevin replied.

The embalming room was nearly silent when Kevin entered. Wearing his surgical coat, latex gloves, and facemask, Boyd stood over Esther's body. Boyd's wise eyes looked past Kevin's, as if trying to determine exactly how much Kevin knew about her.

There was something about Esther that struck Kevin—something that wasn't as noticeable in his first meeting with her but of which was now immediately recognizable and understandable: her cheeks. Her facial muscles around them were still tight, as if they were frozen. He first noticed them in the hospital, after Esther had closed her eyes and hummed a song. Her cheeks, Kevin thought, were conditioned by a lifetime of smiles, millions of smiles, lots of laughter, on a regular basis. And she would be taking them, still intact, to her grave.

"Did you know her?" Kevin asked.

Boyd lowered his mask. "Etty Best. Colorful, vibrant lady. She was the talk of the town, in her day, at least in certain circles." He whispered, as if trying to hide his voice from the corpse, "Some of the guys used to call her 'Easy Etty.'" He resumed a normal tone and began, "You know your father..." then stopped himself and glanced at Kevin. "Never mind," he said as he started to put the mask back into place.

"Yeah, I know, Boyd. She told me the other day."

Boyd stopped, letting the mask drop again. "She told *you*?"

"Yeah, she said they were two sex-starved yachts sharing the harbor for a while."

Boyd erupted with laughter, bringing himself nearly to tears. "That sounds like Etty. What a treasure!"

"I have her music here on my phone."

Kevin repeated the names that Esther had given him: Holiday, Keys, Jones, Fitzgerald, Gardot.

"Lovely, lovely," Boyd remarked with appreciation, "Some classic singers in there. You know about Holiday? Overcame a horrific, horrific childhood. Grew up in a whorehouse. Became one of the more influential musicians of her time. Outspoken, too. Way ahead of her time. But drugs and alcohol ate her alive, destroyed her career, killed her. Died of liver cirrhosis when she was only forty-four."

He walked to his computer, scrolled through his database of music, made a few quick selections and saved them to a playlist. "Let's see now, Billie Holiday...," he said as he promptly started the playlist despite Kevin standing in the room.

"Sorry about the music, Kevin," he apologized, "I know you don't like me playing it while you're in the room, but I've got a few bodies to get through here. Gonna be a busy day."

Years ago, Boyd had tried headphones upon Kevin's request, to respect Kevin's views regarding standards of professionalism. The attempt lasted less than one day: Boyd said that he needed to feel the music, in the room, bouncing off the walls, floor, and ceiling, vibrating through the air. "Headphones," he concluded, "only stifle some of the best qualities of sound." He was not the type to succumb to an earpiece. It wasn't that he was old-fashioned, rather it was because he thought that those devices reduced the power of music. Boyd's embalming rooms, therefore, were perhaps among the very few in the world that were equipped with state-of-the-art surround sound.

As Boyd resumed his work, Kevin heard the sound of a piano, trickling short notes throughout the room. The recording itself was brittle compared to the crisp, clearer modern tracks. Kevin guessed the antique sound was probably from around the 1940s. A soft trumpet purred along with the piano, leading a mature, steady, female singer's voice, the ensemble accompanied by a barely noticeable slow-jazz drumbeat. It was a melancholy song, about the woman's longing for cherished places of her past.

Boyd began to hum along to the music as he worked on Esther's face, hiding the slit along her jugular vein that he had used during the embalming process. Kevin felt the music thumping in his head, worse than it had ever been. He felt himself getting dizzy, swaying a bit in the room. He figured that the sensation must be due to the aftermath of the crash, or side effects of the painkillers, or a combination of both.

Holiday's voice strolled through the first verse and into the second, sharing some of her favorite memories as her accompanying band delivered their notes.

Kevin lost his train of thought as he felt his body begin to make odd, uncontrollable movements. It was as if some mysterious force was sending charges throughout him, jarring his limbs like a throttling, unsteady heartbeat.

What's going on?! Maybe my blood is having some weird reaction to the medication?

He braced himself, trying to hold his arms still by his sides, looking straight down at his legs. The pulsating sensation only intensified, creating even more movement, spreading to his shoulders and hips. This couldn't be something from the medicine alone; there was something about the music. It was the rhythm. Perhaps from all the trauma, his loathing for music was about to send him over the edge.

Oh God, I'm going into convulsions!

He had to get away from that music as quickly as possible. He had to get the hell out of that room, close the door behind him, and find a quiet place where he could get this thing under control.

"Okay, I'm heading to my office," Kevin said as he turned towards the door, "You got everything you need?"

"Kevin?" Boyd called assertively, halting his progress to the door.

Kevin looked hopelessly towards Boyd, his arms and legs gyrating along to the rhythm of Billy Holiday's "I'll Be Seeing You."

"You don't look so good," Boyd said, interrupting his work. He withdrew his mask and stared at Kevin with concern.

"It just started," Kevin said with exasperation. "Must be the painkillers."

Boyd's jaw suddenly dropped. "Wait a minute," he said, "Why are you *dancing*?"

"Dancing? What? No…"

"You're dancing. I've never seen you dance before. Why are you dancing?"

Kevin faced Boyd and let his arms and legs do what they may. He watched his own arms, legs, hips, and feet. Boyd was right: there was some kind of flow to the movement that sort of went along with the song. He was...*dancing!*

"Oh no, Boyd, you've got to help me. I *am* dancing! Something's wrong! Something is *really* wrong!"

Boyd replied with a hint of irritation, "Are you mocking me and my music? Is this because I turned it on while you're still in the room?"

"No, Boyd! Really! I'm dancing, and it won't stop!"

Boyd watched Kevin's movements, as if trying to determine if he was telling the truth. He turned to his computer and stopped the playlist. Immediately, the pulsating charges disappeared from Kevin's body.

Kevin hugged himself, gripped his motionless legs, and exhaled a relieved laugh. He and Boyd stood still, staring at each other in confused silence. Kevin raised his arms, inspecting them for any further signs of uncontrolled motion.

Boyd frowned, drew his eyebrows in contempt and asked, "Are you mocking me?"

"Oh, thank God!" Kevin said, "I don't know what just happened, but thank God that's over!"

He turned towards the door again, satisfied of his body's return to normalcy.

By the time Kevin had taken his third step, however, Boyd had resumed playing the music, this time louder, as if to torment Kevin during his exit. Curious, Kevin stopped. It was a different song. It was another woman's voice, unleashing a scat arrangement along to a jumpy mix of brass and string instruments. A piano and drums rounded out the song. The first few lines were a jumble of *ya-ba-da-ba, dee-ba-dee-ba-doo, hee-ba-doo-be-dah*.... His arms and feet remained still.

Must have been something weird, only for that one song. Whew!

Satisfied, he took a step towards the door.

That is, he *tried* to take a step.

In mid-stride, Kevin's left leg jerked outward and landed flatly, sending a wave of motion through his spine and neck. His hips shook side to side. His arms rose slightly, swinging him into a 180-degree rotation, immediately followed by his right leg landing and sending him into a complete 360-degree rotation.

"Ohhh," he pleaded, "Boyd, help!"

Kevin's chin slightly jerked upwards as his body leaped forward, off his right foot, landing on his left. He spun around another 180-degrees and leaped again, this time with his arms swinging to the beat of the drums.

The woman's sound had its way with him, peppering him with volleys of scat-jazz.

"I knew it!" Dooley exulted as he entered the room and noticed Kevin's dancing. "I've always known you were gay!"

"What?" Kevin gasped between pirouettes.

"It's about time you came out!"

"Dooley!" Kevin blurted as he tip-toed in a circle, his momentum nearly causing him to fall backwards, "I'm not gay! I just can't stop! I don't know what's going on!"

Boyd stopped the music again. As the room fell silent, Kevin nearly collapsed, reaching for a wall to help him retain his balance. With his mouth agape, Boyd stood with his fingers hovering precariously above the computer keyboard as he watched Kevin. Kevin regained his footing and straightened upright as he fought to catch his breath.

"What on Earth?" Boyd muttered to himself, baffled.

Kevin noticed the sinister look in Boyd's eyes; apparently the elder man had realized Kevin was at the mercy of the music. "No, Boyd, please," Kevin begged as he watched Boyd's tempted fingers aim towards the keyboard.

"Yes," Boyd said with a mischievous grin, "Ella Fitzgerald can have that effect on people. I should have known 'Blue Skies' would break your curse."

Before Kevin could respond, Boyd's fingers set the music—and thus Kevin's body—back in motion.

"No, no, please!" Kevin shouted as his body pulsed to the beat of the music, his tapping feet mirroring the skedaddling notes, mercilessly carrying his body across the room.

Again, Boyd halted the music. Kevin stumbled to the floor.

"See?" Dooley remarked, "You've been holding it in too long! You've been trying to hide it so long, that now it's got your head all messed up!"

"No, Dooley," Kevin replied as he gathered himself. "No, it's not that. It's something else. Something is really wrong."

Boyd laughed. "I disagree," he stated calmly. "I don't think you've ever been better."

"Listen," Kevin said, "I'm just going to go home, go back to bed, get some more rest, like the doctor told me to do. If you need me, you know where to find me."

FIVE

The impromptu dance recital in the embalming room happened on Wednesday. Kevin spent the rest of that day and most of Thursday resting and sleeping in silence. Despite the recent boost in business, he had since only called the funeral home twice to check on things.

By Thursday evening, he had become so curious as to whether his condition had disappeared or not that he couldn't help himself. All day long he had resisted the urge to turn on his stereo and subject himself to the effects of music. He never played music on his stereo; he used it exclusively for news, sporting events, and talk shows. He hadn't set its dial to a music station in years.

As the hours of that Thursday passed in his house, the idle, silent stereo seemed to gradually assume a looming, taunting persona, whose presence became increasingly pronounced with each minute. On several occasions that afternoon, Kevin sat on the couch, directly across from it in his living room, resisting the temptation to test it.

By seven p.m., he was feeling brave. At least that's what he'd convinced himself. He'd been staring at the stereo for twenty minutes, debating, flexing his muscles, and practicing holding his arms and legs perfectly still. He hadn't taken his medication at all that day; he would rather deal with the aches than try to tolerate any side effects that produced a rhythmic influence over his limbs, if that was in fact being caused by the medication. The bottle certainly didn't have any indication of such a side effect. Nevertheless, he wasn't taking any chances.

He'd had plenty of sleep. He was well rested. He'd eaten his favorite meals for lunch and dinner—primarily because they were easy enough for a bachelor with limited culinary training to prepare: a corned-beef Reuben sandwich and chicken parmesan, respectively. He capped his dinner off with a delicious, semi-moist brownie with walnuts and a cup of coffee. He was not under any influence whatsoever: he hadn't had any alcohol or drugs. He hadn't had any weird diet drinks like that kale, spinach, and pomegranate mix that once caused him to hallucinate about talking faces on his fingers.

At seven p.m., he was himself. As far as he was concerned, it was just him, Kevin McCormick, slayer of all banal pop culture creations: the true clean force of mankind against the depravity of music.

It was time.

He walked to the stereo, steadying his hands, and turned it on. The first sounds were of voices from a sports talk show, one of Kevin's usual programs. The bitter show hosts were speculating about which Red Sox players were causing the most disruption in the clubhouse, and they were attributing the latest slide in the team's performance to the manager's inability to corral his players.

No music at all. Nothing.

Kevin took a deep breath and hit the "seek" button. He took a step back, into the middle of the room, his fists clenched as he stared in anticipation at the stereo. Scratches and noise sounded from the speakers as the stereo's display panel flickered calling numbers of stations just out of reception. Kevin swore for a moment that the stereo was laughing at him. He relaxed his shoulders and closed his eyes.

Nothing's going to happen. *Nothing.*

Finally, the sound of a buzzing synthesizer along with a forceful drumbeat erupted from the speakers. Kevin had recognized the sound, as he had heard the song at some point just about everywhere: walking through the mall, putting gas in his car, visiting his doctor, and even once crossing paths with a kayaker while canoeing along the Saco River. Secluded hiking trails and rivers nestled in the mountains of New Hampshire were among his favorite escapes from urban commotion...and from pop music. That day on the Saco River, however, he felt violated as the kayaker skimmed passed him, bouncing up and down in his kayak, rowing along to the beat, blasting the sounds of his radio so loud that it seemed to reverberate from the trees that lined the river. Kevin remembered how his skin crawled that summer day as he listened to the kayaker's radio polluting the otherwise perfectly fresh, clear, quiet New Hampshire mountain air. It was Lady Gaga's "Just Dance."

As much as he especially disliked these types of artists, most known for both chasing and defining pop art itself, they were impossible to ignore. Even the most reputable news outlets typically opened their roundup of top stories with updates on these particular celebrities, and Lady Gaga seemed to be one among news networks' chief concerns: what she was wearing, what she wasn't wearing, where she was playing, who she was with, who she wasn't with, what she was eating, what she thought about the weather.

Describing her urge to dance, Gaga's voice bounced from the walls of Kevin's living room.

It was only fitting, Kevin thought, that he would break his new dancing curse against perhaps the ultimate contemporary exploiter of popular art, and also to what he felt was perhaps one of the worst songs in years. "Just Dance" had absolutely no poetic merit whatsoever, he believed, and it contained the simplest of melodies, with a childlike arrangement of only a few basic notes, requiring barely any singing capability at all.

Nothing was happening. He smiled. He had vanquished Lady Gaga. It was over.

Until he reached for the power button.

No sooner was his arm outstretched than it had lurched backward. In one fluid motion his elbow bent as if the music had literally hooked it, followed by a jerky chain reaction from his neck, along his shoulders, down his back, and into his hips. Kevin gasped as his feet took over from there, pitter-pattering in a senseless pattern coordinated only by the notes of the song, his arms abandoning all decorum, recklessly joining the rhythm.

He was petrified.

His feet suddenly shifted together and sent him hopping along to the chorus. He had no control of what or where his body was going. Each time the movement carried him closer to the stereo, he could only helplessly stare at the power button, as his arms and hands worked from a mind of their own. He was certain that he was going to die. He imagined his mother and Boyd preparing his obituary, trying to figure out the best way to explain what had happened. They would never understand.

Cause of death: dancing to Lady Gaga.

The only way out of this, he thought, was to hang on until the song ended; perhaps there would be a silent pause before the next one. He closed his eyes, tried to block out the music as best he could, and prayed to God to spare his life.

Sure enough, his prayers were answered, and the song finally ended. The DJ began to regurgitate Lady Gaga's recent Tweets. Sweating and panting as he crawled across the floor, Kevin took advantage of the merciful break to punch the power button, silencing the stereo. He fell onto his back, fighting for air. He watched the stereo and speakers in terror, as if it might suddenly burst into sound again. With a sudden revelation about how to prevent another episode, he lunged forward and yanked out the stereo's power cord.

As soon as he could speak, but still breathing laboriously, he called 9-1-1. A middle-aged woman's voice responded, "9-1-1, what is your emergency?"

"I'm dancing. I can't stop dancing," Kevin wheezed.

"Excuse me?"

"I'm dancing. Out of control. I need an ambulance."

"You're dancing?"

"Yes."

"And you need an ambulance for that?"

"Yes, right away, please."

Pause. "Is this some kind of a prank, sir? 9-1-1 is for real emergencies only."

"I know, I know, it sounds crazy, but this is a real emergency. Please."

Longer pause. "Have you been drinking, sir?"

"No, no, no. Nothing like that."

"Have you been taking any kind of drugs or medication?"

"No, I'm telling you, this is serious. I need help, right away."

"Are you a mental patient, sir?"

"No, no!" Kevin said, raising his voice. "You don't understand! I hate music! I really hate music! I don't dance! At all! But now I can't stop dancing! Listen to me! My body is doing it all on its own!"

The woman sighed as if irritated. "All right, I'm listening. I'm sorry: did you say you hate music?"

"Yes."

"Well," she murmured, "maybe you should be in jail for that."

"What did you say?"

"Nothing."

"Please! I was just dancing to Lady Gaga!"

"That's not a problem, sir. Lots of people do that every day. I am actually a Lady Gaga fan myself. But, please, try to remain calm. I am trying to help you. Now, I'm assuming you're not in any physical danger at the moment?"

"No, not unless I start to hear music again. You've got to believe me: I could have been killed!"

"'Killed,' sir? By what?"

"By Lady Gaga's song. Or any song!"

"All right. Then I'm sending over a cruiser first. Just sit tight. Block your ears or something, and find a quiet closet or something. Someone is on the way to help."

*   *   *

The sequence of events that followed the "Just Dance" incident not only drowned Kevin deeper into humiliation, but they also escalated his desperation for an explanation. First, two police officers arrived at his home. One introduced himself as Officer Trent, the other as Sergeant Bair. There couldn't have been a less understanding combination of cops for Kevin to explain his problem. Bair, an older, stern-looking man perhaps in his fifties, started the conversation by informing Kevin that prank-calling 9-1-1 could lead to his arrest. Then he began questioning Kevin, while the macho Trent, a much younger black-haired man with the physique of a linebacker, poked around, likely seeking signs of alcohol or drugs. Kevin asserted that he did not have a history of mental illness, and that co-workers at the funeral home witnessed his first dancing attack. The questions evolved into what felt like an interrogation.

"Our dispatcher mentioned something about Lady Gaga," Bair inquired at one point, "Have you ever stalked any celebrities? Threatened them in any way?"

"No. What are you talking about?" Kevin pleaded.

Trent returned from his hunt. "This is incredible," he concluded, "This guy doesn't have anything that would indicate he's any kind of Lady Gaga freak. Sarge, he doesn't even have a single musical item anywhere: no iPhone, CDs, instruments, nothing."

"That's what I've been telling you: I don't listen to music," Kevin said.

"Is that why you dislike Lady Gaga?" Bair asked.

53

"Yes!"

Bair jotted something down in his notepad.

"Look, I'm not a psychopath. I just need to see a doctor," Kevin explained.

"Then why didn't you just drive yourself to the hospital?" Bair asked.

"Because, if I hear music, I go out of control. If someone pulls up next to me and blasts their music, who knows what's going to happen."

"So, then, you're dangerous to people who are playing music?" Bair pressed.

"Yes. I mean, no, no. Not the way you're thinking. The music is dangerous to me. It makes me do things out of my control, so there's no telling what I might do."

Bair looked towards his partner. "Do you have any of that music on your phone?"

"Yes, sir," Trent replied. He reached into his uniform and withdrew his personal phone.

Kevin did find it peculiar that the muscle-bound Trent so readily admitted to having Lady Gaga music on his phone, but he overlooked that curiosity quickly. Right now he just wanted it to convince these officers that he needed help.

Trent tapped the screen of his phone a few times, slid his fingers across it, probably scrolling through apps, before finally holding the phone outward, its speaker aimed at Kevin. The cop's phone began to bombard Kevin with the snapping percussion and whining, buzzing synthesizer hum of Gaga's "Paparazzi."

It took a few seconds, but it wasn't long before Kevin's body contorted, twisting similar to a winding rubber band, then suddenly recoiled and twisted again into the opposite direction. The policemen each rested their hands near their gun holsters, readying for defense.

"Help!" Kevin shouted, clearly in pain as a wrenching twist sent his body into a spin.

The twisting movement paused, but the musical assault over Kevin's body did not: notes began to tear through his body, rapid-fire, like bullets riddling a target.

"Please! Enough!" he begged.

The cops' disposition changed as they watched in astonishment. Trent looked towards Bair for direction. Perplexed, Bair shrugged his shoulders and turned his palms upwards. Bair's face expressed a mournful pity, while Trent's reflected offended disgust.

"Turn it off! Turn it off!" ordered Kevin.

The command broke Trent's appalled glare. He quickly raised the phone to his face and turned it off.

The commotion in Kevin's arms and legs ceased at once. The room fell silent except for Kevin's heavy breathing.

"That's not dancing," Trent finally broke the dead air, "I don't know *what* that was, but it's not dancing."

"Bair here," the other cop spoke into his portable police radio while watching Kevin with apprehension, "We need an ambulance. Right away."

*   *   *

At the hospital, the embarrassment only compounded. In the emergency room, Kevin was sure that the staff was using him for entertainment. What started out with only a nurse and doctor stopping and starting music on their phones to see what would happen—for a variety of songs, which Kevin felt was unnecessary—evolved into a team of six nurses and three doctors gathered around his bedside. Some were gawking, most were trying to stifle snickers, and a few were blatantly laughing. Several patients and a few other hospital workers also matriculated. At least one person appeared to be recording Kevin's jumps and jives, and exclaimed that he was going to make Kevin famous on YouTube.

A younger female nurse echoed Trent's assessment, "I wouldn't call it dancing."

Finally, one of the senior doctors isolated Kevin to his own room, where he remained safe as the hospital administered a series of tests: another CT scan of his head and neck, several MRIs, blood tests, a CSF (cerebral spinal fluid) collection, and even an EMG (electromyogram) to test for potential nerve diseases. After several hours of needles, screens, machines, and numerous medical explanations, Kevin lost track of everything they'd done. A nurse informed him that they would not have all the test results that day, but that a team of doctors was discussing his case and that one of them would be in shortly to discuss "everything" with him.

"Shortly" apparently meant four-and-a-half more hours, when the doctor finally arrived in his room.

"Kevin, I'm Doctor Richards," the scrawny, long-haired man greeted him.

They shook hands.

"I'm one of the doctors on call this evening, but it also happens that I'm somewhat of a nerve specialist."

The doctor explained that he understood that Kevin had recently been through a physically and emotionally traumatic event, but all of the test results that were related to signs of physical damage came back irrefutably negative. There were still a couple of items that were not yet ready, but he didn't expect them to indicate anything different from what they already had shown. Based on what he had seen, Richards concluded that the dancing episodes were related to one of two possibilities: the first was that Kevin had some unique, advanced case of RLS— restless leg syndrome—with episodes induced by audible rhythmic sensations. Richards explained that he had several other patients with RLS, and nearly all of them described a sudden increase in the stress level of their lives, similar to the roller coaster of stress that Kevin had been experiencing since his father died.

"But," the doctor emphasized, "I have never, ever, encountered a case of RLS quite as unique and severe as yours, which leads me to my second, more likely, diagnosis: some form of PTSD."

Post-traumatic stress disorder, or any emotional disorder in that category, was out of the question, Kevin thought.

"I have seen death up close and personal, in countless forms, almost every single day since I was eighteen," Kevin boasted. "I have rarely ever lost sleep over it and have not had a single physical or mental reaction like this to anything, ever. I have gotten over the accident, and have no problems re-living it. Watch..."

He positioned his hands as if they were holding a steering wheel and proceeded to re-enact his car crash, complete with sound effects. The doctor watched with patient indifference.

"See?" Kevin said after explaining how he awoke with a welt on his head, "Nothing. It's music. Just music. When I hear music, it triggers something."

The doctor didn't argue. Instead, he gave Kevin a prescription for drug to treat RLS and told him to avoid music as much as possible. In addition, he handed him a business card for a PTSD therapist.

"If you don't see any improvement after following the prescription for twenty-four hours, call me. Either way, I suggest, firmly, that you make an appointment with a therapist. Immediately."

SIX

Nearly two days on the RLS drug proved only that it had no effect on controlling Kevin's dancing. And that was after even doubling the dose without asking for the doctor's permission.

With Esther's wake approaching, Kevin had discovered a few odd things about his new ailment. First, his body's reaction to rhythm was not immediate: he would have a few seconds after the music started before it completely overwhelmed his body. Second, the seriousness of the effects seemed to be correlated with the level of volume: the louder the music, the more pronounced the movements. He assumed that if he were at a rock concert, for example, he would be completely out of control. If it was playing as soft background music in a mall or quiet restaurant, he could still go about his business, walking and shopping, as his body experienced a mild but continuous dancing seizure. If the music was quiet enough, he didn't have much of a problem turning it off as long as it remained barely audible. Rather, it was a certain decibel level that appeared to send him into what he labeled as "crisis" mode: the point of no return, at which he had no control over himself other than shouting for help.

Some of this he learned by accident while watching television with Dooley. After the two men drew some conclusions about the significance of the level of volume, they decided to experiment in public. They visited a shopping mall, where Kevin managed to spend an hour unscathed other than countless gawks and stares by people who noticed his subtle, continuous, jerky movements. One cashier noted that "My grandmother has Parkinson's, too. Hang in there!"

They ate in a restaurant, again successful except for stabbing himself in the face with a fork and spilling some soup from his spoon. Kevin left the restaurant ecstatic and emboldened, so they visited a nearby Starbucks, which usually had music playing loud enough that you could barely carry a conversation.

Four hesitant steps into the coffee shop, unfortunately, it was over. The shop was playing Danny Fallon's "Littleneeda," and Kevin was pleasantly surprised for all of the first five seconds to find that his body was barely reacting. Suddenly, however, he broke into a step-and-glide groove, one arm aiming forward as he slid across the room, ending with a herky-jerky mess, then back across the room with the other arm outstretched, his palm waving as if clearing his path.

The Starbucks staff appeared to be embracing his act, but the customers didn't seem to know how to react. Some smiled, some clapped to the beat, and some told him to stop trying to cut the line.

Dooley could have asked the employees to stop the music at any time, but he was thoroughly enjoying the desperate looks from Kevin, especially when one of the younger female staff members, probably a college student in her early twenties, decided she was going to dance with him. She raced around the counter, into a similar step-glide, and did her best to copy Kevin's moves across the floor.

"Wow! You're so instinctive! So natural!" she told him.

The slim, curly-haired brunette reached for his hand. As if on impulse, his hand seized hers, and instantly his arm whipped her into a twirl. As she spun, he glided around her. As she slowed he wrapped an arm around her, swinging her off-balance, and leaning her slightly backward.

The song ended. Kevin reached around her with his other arm to stop her momentum, the two of them nearly falling to the floor. With both arms he yanked her upright and returned her to a standing position.

"Wow!" she whispered to him, her eyes gazing at his in disbelief, "You're amazing!"

The break in the music allowed Kevin to regain his composure. He turned and hurried for the door as the entire crowd, including the staff, applauded. Once outside, Kevin rested his hands on his knees, bending over to catch his breath.

Dooley followed him through the door. "Kev, man, that was awesome! They're going nuts in there!" He patted Kevin on the back.

The brunette suddenly rushed past the door, following Dooley.

"Hey," she said to Kevin, handing him a small paper, "I've got to get back to work, but call me if you want to go dancing sometime!"

Kevin tried to respond, but his jaw was frozen.

"Call me, okay?" she smiled, "I love a good dance partner." She blew him a kiss and skipped merrily back into the shop.

The two men stood, staring at the door as it closed behind her.

"Did you see that?!" Dooley finally broke the silence.

"Yes," Kevin angrily replied, "That wasn't me that grabbed her though. That was something else. Lucky all I did was twirl her and swing her around."

"Are you kidding? They were cheering you in there!"

"Dooley . . . do you understand that the wrong dance moves in there could have gotten me arrested?"

"Yeah, but Kevin, think about this: whoever thought that chicks would dig *you* because of music?"

Kevin knew exactly what Dooley was talking about: music had only led to the demise of some of his most serious relationships with women. At his high school prom, his date was swept off her feet by the breakdancing moves of Andy "M.C." Jackson. By the time Kevin was a high school senior, the breakdancing trend had long since faded, but that didn't stop M.C.—who arrived stag at the prom—from performing his outdated circus act in front of Lori Kitaen, Kevin's girlfriend of four months. Kevin tried to discourage M.C., telling him to take his freaky scene back to the eighties, only to watch Lori accept M.C.'s offer to dance. Kevin sat alone in helpless misery by the punch bowl, observing as Lori fell hard for the slinky, body-waving, parachute-pants wearing, head-spinning oddity. Lori only spoke to Kevin one other time for the rest of the evening: to tell him thanks for a fun time but she was leaving with M.C.

Kevin never completely recovered from the prom humiliation, but meeting the love of his life—or so he thought at the time—in his first semester of college certainly helped to repair his ego. She was a fellow classmate, Molly Moore, who he met at a college party. From that night forward they were hot and heavy for about eight months, with little interruption from music. They even discussed getting married after college…until Brad Lowe interjected.

Brad shattered Kevin's world late one evening when Kevin and Molly stopped by a quiet café for a cappuccino—their routine Wednesday night rendezvous. Typically there would be some local college rock star wannabe providing some horrible background music from a corner of the café. That particular evening, an unkempt slob with a spotty beard growth of five or six days, wearing sunglasses despite standing in the dimly lit corner at ten p.m., plucked away at an over-abused, out-of-tune guitar that was missing two strings. The sad excuse for a musician's name was Brad Lowe. Brad had a breathy style of singing and held his mouth so close to the microphone that Kevin wondered if he might eat it. He spent more time pushing his long, dirty-blonde hair from his face than playing the guitar. At one point, he even interrupted the song entirely to fix his hair for a few seconds, then continued from the very next note as if nothing had happened.

Somewhere in that mess, Brad came across as a likeable, sensitive, handsome man...at least to the women in the college café.

Brad introduced each of his songs as an "original cry of pain," which was also apparently the title of his new homemade CD. "Here's another original cry of pain," he would say, leading into some long, deep breaths about some incredibly beautiful woman who wouldn't accept him for who he was, broke his heart, left him for some superficial rich guy who didn't understand what life was *really* all about, and how he still had all this love to give...or some bullshit like that.

Kevin thought Brad was ridiculous, pathetic, and above all a horrible musician. On one hand, Kevin couldn't help but laugh at Brad's act, but on the other hand he couldn't help but feel a bit sorry for him.

Naturally, Kevin was stunned when Molly turned to him and whispered, "Isn't he amazing? I think we should talk to him after his set. He's...just...so...brilliant."

At first, Kevin thought Molly was joking. Then, after watching Brad boldly dedicate his final original cry of pain to Molly—whose name he had not yet learned so instead he referred to as "the delicate red-haired angel back there"—Kevin could see that Molly was intrigued, if not enchanted. Nevertheless, certain that she would see through this con man's game, Kevin decided to humor Molly by going with her to talk to Brad after his set. Kevin introduced himself and Molly. Brad never removed the sunglasses.

"That's some...very...powerful stuff you did up there," Kevin remarked.

"Yeah, yeah," Brad replied, staring towards Molly—somewhere, but it was hard to discern exactly where because of the glasses—and shook her hand.

From that moment, the conversation involved Molly and Brad exclusively. It was as if Molly had completely forgotten that Kevin was standing right there. Molly couldn't hide her beaming smile and fixed gaze; it was as if some kind of spell had turned her into a Brad-mesmerized zombie. After about a half hour which included Brad reading Molly's palms and stroking her hair to give her advice on what types of conditioners to use, Kevin simply walked out of the café. He was pretty sure that Molly didn't even realize that he had gone. Nor would he ever hear from Molly again.

Music had unleashed its merciless wave of destruction once again.

But now, as bizarre as it sounded, Dooley's comment at Starbucks—about the newfound musical power Kevin could have over women with this dancing gimmick—resonated with Kevin. After all, it was the first time that a woman had offered her number, unsolicited, to Kevin; maybe Dooley *was* on to something.

After Starbucks, they proceeded more cautiously. They spent the rest of the evening playing with the car stereo, experimenting with various volumes, trying to figure out how the disease worked. As they drove through the town, they tested different locations, poking their heads into stores and restaurants, trying to gauge the level of sound and guessing if it was too dangerous or not.

It was, to say the least, one of the most interesting evenings that either one of them had ever experienced.

*   *   *

By the time Esther's wake began the following afternoon, Kevin and Dooley had devised a plan: they would play the music at the wake so that it was barely audible. Music during the wake was always optional, and some customers did prefer quiet. However, Esther and Amy had requested a very specific set of songs, so there was no getting around that. Kevin would try to avoid being around the music as much as possible. He knew that his staff was perfectly capable of handling things without him, but he still felt a loyal obligation to fulfill his father's commitment to Esther. He also wanted to apologize to Amy for not being around to take her calls when her mother died.

His mother Dotty, in particular, was adamant that Kevin be present to oversee Esther's wake and funeral. She also kept asking, repeatedly, if he had called Amy to see if she needed anything, or at least to ensure her that everything was covered. It felt as though each hour, on the hour, Dotty would ask, "Have you talked to her yet?"

"No, Mom, if there's an issue I will call her. Otherwise, we have it under control."

Nevertheless, Kevin did admit to himself that part of him wanted to see Amy, despite the circumstances. That undoubtedly had something to do with his motivation for getting his dancing illness under control.

Before the wake, as was tradition for similar services at McCormick Funeral Home, family and close friends were given some private time with their loved one before opening the home to other participants. Esther's case was unusual, however, because she had been married four times and was survived by two ex-husbands. Amy was an only child, yet she had an extended family from Esther's other relationships. Most of these people she'd never even met, and the rest she hadn't seen in years, even during Esther's final weeks. She was sadly alone, which was perfect for Kevin: it would provide him with plenty of quiet opportunities to apologize to Amy and extend his condolences. After that, he could virtually disappear without anyone wondering where the funeral director was.

Amy was the last of the private group to arrive. She entered the home very slowly, reluctantly, but—surprisingly—wearing a soft-pink mid-length dress, a white sweater, and white gloves. She held a small black purse in her hand. In a change from her somewhat disheveled appearance when Kevin first met her in the hospital, she'd now had her hair done, probably professionally, and wore a modest matching earring and pendant set. She walked with a graceful gait. Her dark, dreary eyes revealed hours of tears, yet she looked beautiful. When she noticed Kevin standing in a common area outside the viewing room, she changed directions and hastened her paced towards him.

"Oh my God!" she said, noticing the bruises on his face. "Your assistant told me that you were in a car accident, but I had no idea!"

"Yes, earlier this week. I'm sorry I wasn't able to take the call like I had promised."

"Oh, no," she interrupted, "Please don't apologize! I didn't expect you to be here."

"You look amazing." He couldn't help himself in saying so.

"Oh, please," she smiled, "I haven't slept in over a week. The pink: I know it's an odd choice, but Mom hated dark colors. She didn't want me wearing black or gray for this." She shrugged her shoulders.

"No, I understand."

Her smile yielded to anxious, pursed lips as she looked around the room: the flowers, the notes, the pictures.

"I don't know if I can do this," she gasped as she held back her tears and wiped her eyes. "I mean, look at me," she remarked, pointing to her watering eyes.

"Hey," he commented, "You'll get through it. And you look…stunning. Really. I mean—and I never say this to any clients—but it's tough for me to take my eyes off you. Don't worry about how you look."

She laughed, "Isn't that a little inappropriate, given the situation?"

"Yes. Absolutely." He had her laughing, "Completely unprofessional. But something tells me your mother would be telling you the same thing."

She blurted out a laugh that caught everyone's attention.

"Thanks," she said, "I'm going to go..."

Kevin nodded. He watched as Amy turned towards the viewing room. Inside, she stared at Esther in the casket before approaching it. Kevin held his breath as Amy took a deep breath of her own. Esther lay in her favorite baby-blue outfit with a white sweater that matched Amy's. Her thin hands were folded peacefully on her stomach, the casket below her waist closed. Her content face was slightly propped up on a pillow, her hair styled for the last time.

Amy walked slowly towards the casket, knelt beside it, clasped her hands around her mother's, and wept. Ordinarily, Kevin wouldn't watch this; he would wander outside the room, giving people as much time and privacy as possible. But Amy was clearly alone today, and she looked like she was about to collapse next to the casket. He felt some kind of connection to her, an only child himself, having lost his adored father at about the same age. He understood her pain. He felt a responsibility for her, not only because he sympathized with the weight of her loss: the sudden, unavoidable, terminality of her most nurturing relationship.

Kevin had seen this over and over again with clients; no matter how long Esther had been sick, no matter how many potential final goodbyes they had shared, no matter how much they had discussed Esther's death, it was difficult if not impossible for Amy to be prepared for the reality that Esther was gone. There would be no more conversations over a cup of tea, no more silly stories, no more advice, no more embraces. Kevin understood the look in Amy's eyes as she nodded to herself, perhaps trying to accept how much her world had changed. He resisted the urge to enter the room to console her, believing it would be inappropriate and unprofessional. He was relieved to see her finally gather herself, whisper "I love you, Mom," wipe her tears, straighten her posture, and walk out of the room as if she was in complete command of the world.

She was ready now. The worst was over. His job was done. He could run and hide in his quiet office until Esther's service had ended. As Amy exited the viewing room, he was prepared to let her know that Dooley or one of the other staff members would find him if she needed anything else.

"Mr. McCormick," she began.

"Kevin," he corrected her.

She smiled again. "Thanks. Kevin, then…I have something to ask."

"Sure."

"I'm not sure how these things work. I've never been to many, not even my father's, so I'm not even sure if this would be normal."

"Yes?"

"Well, I don't know if I'm up to this today. And I don't really have anyone. These people, they *are* my relatives, but we haven't seen…*any* of them…in years. But you seem so professional, and your company has been so wonderful to us. I know you've probably watched a hundred of these kinds of things."

"Hundreds," he confirmed, nodding confidently. "What is it?"

"You seem like such a strong person, and someone who could handle this, and help me through it. Would it be too out of custom for me to ask you to stand near me, not right next to me of course, but somewhere near, to make sure I get through this?"

No, it was not customary at all, at least at the McCormick Funeral Home. And given the history between Esther and Harry, he wouldn't want to be seen anywhere near the condolence line. Above all, when the wake started, so would the music, and there was no way he could stand in the middle of a room full of mourners while dancing.

"Amy," he shook his head, "I really can't…"

Before he could answer, her legs went limp. Her chin dropped as her purse fell to the floor. She was fainting. He caught her as she completely melted into a flimsy jumble of limbs. Along with Dooley and another staff member named Barry, he helped her to a couch.

The start of the wake was delayed for about twenty minutes as Amy regained her awareness. By the time she had awakened, her request had become an order: "I will need you to stand within a few feet of me." Kevin tried to convince her that Dooley, Barry, or someone else was better suited, but she insisted that it be Kevin. Dooley gave Kevin a wink, letting him know that the music would be barely audible.

As the flow of mourners began, the music played softly, as they had planned. Kevin stood about ten feet from Amy: close enough so that she knew where he was, yet far enough that he wouldn't be mistaken for part of the Best family. Despite the faint sound, Kevin still felt some effects of the music. Nevertheless, at least he wasn't hopping around or gliding across the floor. Instead, he felt that he had some bodily control, albeit shaky control. He also tried to cleverly, continuously shift his stance, in an attempt to shield the pulses that popped from random points of his body along to the melodies.

Every few minutes, between accepting condolences from the train of visitors, Amy would look towards him. At first, her unsteady, tense glances reeked of confusion and puzzlement. As the minutes stretched past the first hour, however, her ganders had evolved into pleasant, appreciative smiles in his direction. A few times she even had to cover her mouth to suppress laughter. He tried desperately to hide his problem, at first trying to hold himself still, putting his arms straight down. Then he gave up and instead tried to make it appear as if the jumpiness was natural and intended. Nothing seemed to work, and although he was a safe distance away from the line, some mourners still went out of their way to make comments to him:

"Are you okay?" and "Hey buddy, lay off the coffee."

A small group of Etty's female neighbors from an elderly housing complex noticed him, told him they liked the song too, and danced while waiting in line.

Kevin couldn't help but notice that the mourners were primarily elderly men. Sure, there were plenty of women and members of the four extended families, but it was impossible to overlook the steady train of men, unaccompanied by wives or significant others. He tried to ignore this oddity, but during one break even Amy herself acknowledged, "Yes, my mom had a bit of a reputation."

As the flow of visitors settled to a trickle, Amy had bigger breaks between each mourner. She approached Kevin and said with a grin, "Thanks, that's just what I needed."

"What?"

"The dancing. I knew you would find a way to get me through."

"Oh, yeah…of course," he muttered, trying uselessly to hold himself still.

"Are you really a Gardot fan?"

"A what?"

"Melody Gardot. This song: 'Who Will Comfort Me.' It's one of her most popular songs. My mom loved it."

"I don't know anything about her."

"My mother found her sound incredibly soothing."

"I guess it is. But I never heard of her."

"Gardot's an amazing story: she was struck by a car while riding a bike. She had some severe spine and brain injuries. A doctor recommended musical therapy to help her recover some of her mental capacity. So she did: she listened to music, started singing jazz, and that played a big role in her recovery. Changed her life completely."

"Musical therapy?"

"Yes. She says it helped her brain regain its function and gave her some general spiritual boost."

Kevin laughed, shaking his head as his shoulders shimmied and his hips gyrated to the song.

"Musical therapy?" he repeated.

"I know, it sounds crazy. But I think there's some truth to it. Like tonight: you were my musical therapy, in a way. My mom never understood why funerals have to be so sad and gloomy and depressing. She was telling me last week that she didn't want everyone to feel sorry for her, because she enjoyed her life. Then, you know, I was watching you...it was like you couldn't help yourself. Like you couldn't stop dancing even if you wanted."

"Amy, all I can say is, you don't even know how true that is."

SEVEN

Kevin couldn't believe his luck at the wake: not only had Amy been unsuspicious of his behavior, but she actually welcomed it. He knew that Esther's funeral wouldn't be so easy. For one thing, he and Dooley wouldn't be able to control the volume of the choir and pipe organ that burst from the balcony of the church. For another, the church ceremony would be more formal than the wake, so dancing along to the music would be unacceptable.

The plan was for Kevin to stay towards the rear of the church, in a foyer area that was separated from the pews by doors. Dooley and Barry would direct things inside the church. Kevin explained to Amy that this is how they normally conducted the funeral because, "If something comes up, it's disrespectful for me to be talking on my cell phone inside the main church." From the back of the church, he could still observe while being able to respond to emergencies. He told her that prior to the end of the church service, he would leave early to go to the burial site before the vehicle procession arrived in order to "make sure that everything is okay." Amy bought the explanation.

The church service was much more challenging than Kevin had anticipated: he had never noticed how much music was involved in these events, perhaps because over the years he had become so proficient at blocking it out. Kevin tried to wait in the foyer area between the closed doors to the pews and the exterior doors, thinking that he probably wasn't going to hear much there.

He was dead wrong. The first time the organ exploded into "Jesus Christ Is Risen Today," his body jumped into action, the notes sending him spinning and swinging in random directions. Luckily the hymn had lots of pauses, permitting Kevin many chances to rest. Coming out of each pause, however, the first few thundering notes were the worst, jolting his entire frame. The organ did not have any accompaniment, which helped to make the music overall less taxing on him. Nevertheless, it felt like three minutes of electric shock torture by pipe organ.

The foyer doors had glass windows: something both he and Dooley had overlooked. After the opening hymn ended, Kevin tried to find a place which would leave him least prone to being seen once the music resumed. Still, there was no way to predict where his body would eventually go.

The second song was Franz Shubert's "Ave Maria." The organ announced its presence with a brief introduction before the choir joined. Again, Kevin fell into a reckless trance of leaps and spins. At the end of each line, his body would launch itself across the small room, sometimes landing him harmlessly in the middle, other times sending him crashing into a wall or post. At one point he even crashed into the doors themselves. Luckily everyone in the church except for the priest was facing directly away from Kevin's dance floor.

The second time he crashed into the doors, however, he could see some of the mourners towards the back of the church turn around to see what was happening. The people that noticed tapped the shoulders of others near them, until about twenty guests were watching him. Because they only had a partial view through the doors' windows, Kevin was certain that they couldn't tell exactly what was happening. Still, he knew that after one more song like this, the entire congregation would figure out what was going on with the funeral director in the foyer.

Why does this organist have to play with so much energy? This is a funeral!

As soon as the song ended, he thought, he would escape to the outside of the church and wait there until the next stage of the funeral. If he dared to subject himself to another song, one of these crazy leaps was going to result in him breaking something in the church, or himself, or both.

As the heads continued to rotate towards the ruckus in the foyer, he could see Dooley occasionally turn his attention towards the back of the church, concerned for him.

"Benedicta tu in mulieribus... "

Kevin's body leaped against a flower vase supported by a column. The entire fixture came crashing down onto him, sending a pool of water and flowers across the foyer. Before he had a chance to notice his drenched left pant leg, the next line had begun, and he was off into another direction.

"Et benedictus
Et benedictus fructus ventris... "

As the music swung Kevin's body past a window, he was able to get a glimpse of Amy, seated towards the front of the church in her yellow dress. Her head was momentarily turned towards the back of the church, as if discreetly looking for Kevin. As she dabbed her eyes with a tissue, she noticed him leap past another window.

Although it was one of his better leaps—arms outstretched, chest out, chin up, overall decent form—Kevin was helplessly embarrassed. There was no hiding this from Amy, as his body hurled itself into motion, at the mercy of the music. The notes themselves were not physically abusive; it was rather that nearly every line ended with a violent launch.

Finally, it stopped. Kevin collapsed to the floor, below the level of the windows, where he was certain nobody could see him. Before he crawled outside to safety, he couldn't help but move closer to the door to get a peek through the glass.

He peered carefully over the bottom of a window, only enough so that one eye could see into the church. The elderly priest, who hadn't seemed to notice any of the commotion, had simply resumed the prayers. The other people seated toward the back—those of whom Kevin had attracted attention—were now all facing forward, joining the praying. Dooley was trying to face forward as well.

The one person who still had her head partially turned in his direction was Amy. Evidently, she had spotted Kevin's eye peeking through the window. As they caught each other's eye—or, rather, Amy's eyes caught Kevin's eye—she very subtly raised the fingers of one of her white gloves.

She can see me?!

His embarrassment was growing by the second.

To his surprise, however, as she concluded her barely noticeable wave, she gave him one of her bright, beaming smiles and mouthed, "Thank you!"

She continued to stare in his direction. He stood upright, moving so that she could see him in full view through the window. He gave her a confident nod, implying that he knew what he was doing and had everything under control. He pointed to her emphatically and gestured with his thumb and index finger "okay." He had no idea that blood was trickling from a new gash in his forehead.

She nodded, smiled, and turned her attention back towards the altar.

Kevin raced through the exterior doors before the next song began. There, he was safe from musical infection as the ceremony continued. Before the Mass had completely ended, he fled to the cemetery, where he had previously told Amy he would be.

At the graveside service, where the mourners said their very final respects before the casket is lowered into the ground, Kevin remained in one of his company's cars, also as he had planned. There would be bagpipes played at some point during the portion of the funeral, and they would be earth-shattering, so Kevin wanted to make sure he was in a secure place.

Inside the car, he sat in the back seat, where the tinted windows would ensure that no one outside could see him. He confirmed that the windows and doors were sealed shut. He watched nervously, waiting for the pipers' moment. When it began, he muffled his ears as best he could, with whatever he could find.

He learned something then: the sound of bagpipes can pierce *anything*.

Dooley would later describe to Kevin that the bagpipes were so loud that you couldn't hear Kevin slamming around in the back seat of the car. In fact, Dooley said, most of those who made it to the cemetery didn't notice anything at all. Even those who *did* notice couldn't see Kevin, Dooley explained: they could only see a black Lincoln sedan bouncing uncontrollably, up and down, back and forth.

When the music stopped, Dooley said he whispered to them, "My dog. Bagpipes get him excited."

When it was over, Kevin was too embarrassed to step outside the car. Dooley anticipated this and simply told Amy that he thought Kevin must have gone already; he had to get back to the home for another service. Amy had a message for Dooley to deliver to Kevin: "Please tell him I said thanks for keeping my spirits up, the way my mom would have wanted. She would have been thrilled to know that someone actually danced during her funeral."

As they drove back to the home and recapped the events of the past two days, Dooley had his own message for Kevin, "Dude, you need to see a shrink. You're a mess. And you might not survive this."

EIGHT

Kevin's first experience with psychiatry was probably going to be his last, he'd decided, after an hour with a therapist. Dr. Susan Bowman was friendly, in her fifties, with short, wavy hair, and other than her brown-plaid dress, she was about as plain and stoic a person as Kevin had ever met. She wore no makeup, had no eyelashes, and hardly a trace of eyebrows. Her eyes were buried deep inside their sockets: brownish-black dots in the shadows of two tunnels below her huge forehead. He couldn't help but think of how much she reminded him of his high school hockey coach. She wore white pumps with no stockings. No jewelry. Not even fingernail polish. There were no pictures in her office: only light gray walls. Her furniture and carpet were a slightly darker shade of gray that matched the walls. She had one window, which overlooked the brick side of the building next door.

Dr. Bowman greeted Kevin warmly, gently shaking his hand and smiling. She offered him water and gave him the option to sit in a lounge chair or a small sofa. He took the chair. They made some small talk about the weather, the traffic, and how long it took him to get there. They exchanged observations about the neighborhood in which she maintained her office. At first, Kevin felt comfortable; she was generic, but nice.

The first few minutes of the session were as generic as Dr. Bowman. Kevin answered basic questions about his health, the car accident, his work, relationships with co-workers, his father's death, and his day-to-day activities outside of work. She asked for specifics about his dancing ailment: what parts of his body moved the most, in what directions. Was it a certain style or mix of styles? Which particular music caused what? Kevin explained how his body responded according to the level of volume. He described how his body, independently as if possessed by some dancing spirit, lifted and spun the young woman in the coffee shop. He told her how he had danced through Esther's entire wake. He explained how he nearly split his head open while leaping across the church foyer and crashing into the standing vase during "Ave Maria." This was all information which Kevin had expected to provide.

To observe the problem herself, the doctor requested that Kevin perform in the middle of the room, along to what she proclaimed to be "one of the great musical arrangements of all time" which turned out to be a remake version of "Muskrat Love" by the 1970s duo Captain and Tennille. Kevin wondered what could possibly have been wrong in the world in 1976, which Bowman insisted was the year when the song spent four weeks as the number-one hit in the United States.

"Muskrat Love" was a charming, childlike melody about two rodents enjoying a sexual frolic, complete with giggling and foreplay. Kevin was mentally paralyzed as the doctor reminisced with proud delight about how Captain and Tennille once performed it at the White House for Queen Elizabeth II. Thankfully, the dance this time wasn't too physically challenging. There weren't too many athletic moves, only some simple motions using his arms, with a few head jerks and pirouettes. The worst of it was the shivering that went along with the keyboard's special muskrat-purring sound effects.

Then things got weird.

Bowman started asking about the women in his life, of which currently there was really only Dotty. Kevin had had girlfriends in the past, but his longest relationship was eight months. He briefly explained how he lost one serious girlfriend to a breakdancer and another to a so-called musician who more closely resembled a mop. His grandparents had all died before he was ten. No sisters. There were only a few female employees at the home over the years, but he was never very close to any of them. And he just hadn't had many female friends.

The doctor seemed extremely intrigued by this, raising her balding eyebrows, listening intently while pressing a finger to her chin. When Kevin had finished recounting his lack of lasting, meaningful relationships with women, the room fell silent for what felt like an entire, eternal minute.

Finally, the doctor asked, in her nicely stoic delivery, "Let me ask you this, bluntly: do you think your lack of relationships with women is a result of your hidden longings for your mother?"

"Excuse me?" Kevin was sure the doctor had misspoken.

"Your suppressed desires for your mother... that are interfering with your ability to develop any kind of relationships with other women?"

"Excuse me?"

"Have you spoken to your mother about this?"

"Ex... excu... I'm sorry?"

"It's a Freudian view, but one that could be very relevant in your case."

"Excuse me?"

"At what age did your mother stop breastfeeding you?"

"Okay, look, I'm here because I have a dancing problem. It's destroying my life. The reason I never had a relationship work out is because people don't like people who are around dead bodies all the time. And, as *you* can relate, I'm not the most exciting or attractive person either."

Dr. Bowman didn't acknowledge Kevin's explanation. She only maintained her prognosis, saying, very plainly, that she thought the reason Kevin really hated music was because there must have been some musical experience in his past—perhaps Dotty liked to play music while she was breastfeeding him—that he was subconsciously suppressing. This event, or related, repeated events, was contributing to his phobia of music. Bowman said that she believed that now, with Kevin's father out of the picture, it was becoming more difficult for Kevin to suppress these true passions for Dotty; those feelings had become so forcible that they were now manifesting themselves in dance, which was being triggered by music. This was a direct result from the way that the sounds of music, when Kevin was a baby, had conditioned him—intentionally or unintentionally—to have the desire…or need…to be breastfed.

Kevin listened carefully to her entire theory. He sat in the gray chair, arms flat on the armrest, as sweat matted the hair on his forehead. She interrupted her diagnosis twice: once to point out that his posture—hands fiercely clutching the armrests, feet firmly planted, back buried into the chair—indicated that he was seeking security at that very moment, and the second time to suggest that the sweat was being caused by extreme anxiety.

He was stunned, yet fascinated.

Above all, he was appalled.

Satisfied that she had completed her theories and interpretations, Kevin rose from the chair and said calmly, "I'm going to leave now."

"But you still have ten minutes."

"That's okay. You can keep the change."

The doctor ended the session by telling him that it could take anywhere between three to ten sessions, of one hour each, before she could conclusively diagnose his condition and determine the best course of action to treat it. She wanted to spend two to three weeks covering his childhood, another two to three weeks on his adolescence, and yet another two to three weeks discussing his relationships with his parents. At two-hundred and fifty dollars per session.

Alternatively, she offered to accelerate the entire process simply by hypnotizing him for five hundred dollars at the very next session. This would enable her to "quickly get to the heart of the matter, confirm my suspicions, and then we can go from there."

Kevin replied that between his fantasies about his mother and the dancing seizures, he'd try his best to consider her options.

At that time, Dr. Bowman would not prescribe any medication or treatment other than, "Carry a set of ear plugs with you at all times."

It was actually great advice. In fact, he wished then that he'd had a pair for that entire psychiatric evaluation. On his way back to the funeral home from his first and only ever psychiatric therapy session, Kevin stopped at a drug store and bought not one, but five, sets of top-of-the-line earplugs.

NINE

The earplugs were tiny, barely noticeable, and colored to blend with different shades of skin. Despite how well they worked, Kevin was lucky to be alive after the next client.

The services were for a ninety-four-year-old Italian man, Tony Martino, who had died peacefully in his sleep. Tony's family fled Italy just before World War II, while he was in his late teens. Boyd told Kevin that it was rumored that the Martinos were associated with the Sicilian mafia, of which Benito Mussolini was trying to purge Italy at the time. Many of these Italian immigrants ended up in Philadelphia, Chicago, and New York before branching out to Boston and other places. In his twenties, Martino enlisted in the United States Army and actually took part in the invasion of Italy in 1943.

For decades, Martino ran a well-known masonry business in Saugus, an urban, blue-collar town that neighbored Malden. Still, according to Boyd, he could not completely cut ties from his family's mafia roots. When Kevin first asked Gina Martino, Tony's wife, the question—about his favorite music—she burst into a wailing mess as she was sitting in the den of the modest Martino estate. He waited patiently until she calmed down before asking again, "I'm sorry, Mrs. Martino, but I really have to know, for the embalmer."

She exploded into howls of sorrow once again, as a very large man standing by her side said, "Move on, pal. You've got your information, now go do your job."

Kevin whispered to the man, "Is there anyone else who would know?"

The man seized him by the arm, nearly lifting him off the floor, and led him out of the room, saying, "You think this is some kind of joke?!"

The big man's name was Don. He was from New York, and in no way related to the Martinos. Don's job, assigned by "someone who gives orders" as he explained, was to watch over Tony's funeral. This was a first for Kevin. He even helped wheel the body into the embalming room and stood over it until Boyd began the process. Don had a partner named Sal, who was instructed by the person who gave the orders to look after Gina. Neither Don nor Sal liked Kevin, which made it impossible for him to get the answer to the music question.

After listening to Kevin explain this, Boyd decided to do something he rarely did in his career, and never did with a stranger: meet with the family. Boyd wasn't going to take any chances with the person who gives orders. He was going to make sure that Mr. Martino's appearance was exceptional, and for that he needed the music.

Kevin drove. When they arrived at the Martino house, Kevin followed Boyd's lead. This time, cars lined the street in front of the house and around the block. The house was overflowing with guests, flowers, and food. The home was filled with the warm scent of fresh-baked loaves of bread mixed with the aromas of spices—basil, oregano, onion, garlic—from the many pasta dishes that neighbors had delivered. Dozens of vases of roses, poppies, lilies, and violets, offered in sympathy, crowded the doorway and lined the main interior of the home.

As Boyd stepped past the front door, he removed his black trilby hat and walked slowly through the first room, slightly bowing his head towards each person who made eye contact with him. Despite the toll that age had taken over Boyd's spine, at well over six feet tall he still towered over almost everyone there.

Boyd remained silent as he moved through the crowd, flowers, and food, empathetically acknowledging those whose attention he had attracted. Gina Martino was no longer in the den; it had since been overtaken by mourners, food, and flowers. He respectfully, thoughtfully looked into two other rooms in which mourners were gathered before finally spotting Gina. He turned to Kevin for confirmation.

Kevin nodded, "That's her."

They stood in the doorway of what appeared to be some sort of a reading room, where ninety-eight year old Gina, who appeared to be ailing herself, sat in a lounge chair, Sal standing by her side. There were only a handful of other people in this particular room: one very elderly man, two other men and one woman, perhaps all in their sixties, and two other men not much younger than Kevin.

"May I?" Boyd asked Gina, and then glanced towards Sal, who gave him a nod.

Boyd stepped into the room. A few feet away from Gina, he stood still, arms by his sides. Gina was clearly crushed: her thin, wrinkled, veined hands shaking, a sorrowful frown sealed on her face. She looked up at Boyd with her exhausted, broken-hearted eyes.

"Mrs. Martino," Boyd began sincerely, "*Mi chiamo* Boyd Oakley. *Preparo suo marito.*"

He paused before continuing, as if pleading, "*Sig.ra Martino, sono semplicemente uomo. Senza la musica, sono mortale, fallibile, umile, disperato. La musica è la mia finestra all'anima.*" He paused again, looking into her eyes, "*Per favore, consente che io vedere l'anima di suo marito.*"[1]

The words flowed from Boyd beautifully, effortlessly, as if he had been speaking Italian his whole

---

[1] Translation: "My name is Boyd Oakley. I am preparing your husband. Mrs. Martino, I am merely a man. Without music, I am mortal, fallible, meek, hopeless. Music is my window to the soul. Please, allow me to see your husband's soul."

life. Kevin recognized the language, but had no idea what Boyd said. He had no idea that Boyd even spoke Italian. The entire room froze. Whatever he said was powerful: it had even given Sal a lump in his throat.

Gina extended one of her shaking hands. Boyd tucked his hat under his arm and gently sealed his strong hands around hers.

She softly wept as she spoke, barely audible, so that Boyd had to stoop forward until his ear was within about a foot of her mouth, "Martinelli, Pavarotti, Bocelli... Puccini, Giordano...   Fedora, Gianni Schicchi, Madama Butterfly, Turrandot, La Bohème."

Sounded like Italian opera, Kevin guessed. Boyd seemed to know exactly what she was talking about: he did not need to write anything down, nor did he ask for clarification. He simply stood upright, held her hand for a moment, and said, "*Grazie, sono onorato. Ho il grande rispetto per suo marito. Nessun dorma, nessun dorma. Tu pure, o Principessa, nella tua fredda stanza, guardi le stelle che tremano d'amore, e di speranza.*"[2]

"Puccini," she wept as she squeezed his hand, pulled it towards her lips, and gave it a soft kiss.

"*Grazie*, thank you," he said as he released her hand and stepped backward, as if a peasant trying to be careful not to turn his back on royalty.

The curiosity outside the room had drawn the crowd closer to it. When they stepped through the doorway, Kevin was struck by how many people were watching them. Boyd stepped past Kevin and placed his hat on his head. The crowd cleared a path for Boyd, all the way to the front door, as if he was Moses parting the Red Sea.

---

[2] Translation: "Thank you. I am honored. I have great respect for your husband." Quoting Giacomo Puccini's Nessun Dorma: "None shall sleep, none shall sleep. Even you, O Princess, in your cold bedroom, watch the stars that tremble with love and with hope."

Kevin was speechless until they returned to the car, "Where did you learn how to speak Italian?"

"Opera. Lots of opera, over the years. Very educational stuff."

*   *   *

As Boyd worked on the body, Kevin could faintly hear the opera music, despite both his and Boyd's doors being closed. He thought about wearing the earplugs, but then realized this was one sort of music he could almost tolerate. His body mildly rocked and swayed, but he didn't seem to be experiencing any herky-jerky movement or urges to jump or leap. He found that he could sit there, at his desk, with a very good level of control over his limbs, while he continued to watch online videos about how to read lips.

Kevin got the idea about reading lips from talking to Dooley and Boyd about lip-syncing. Dooley was helping Boyd prepare the body of a middle-aged man whose family listed 50 Cent among his favorite musicians. Boyd's view was that lip-sync artists had less talent than musicians who catered their songs to each occasion. Dooley said that it didn't matter to him: sometimes great performers were not exactly great musicians and vice versa, therefore he could understand a production that aimed to capture the best of both worlds while appealing to a certain market. Sometimes the show was as much about the interpreting movement on stage as it was about the song itself, and there was nothing wrong with a theatrical presentation.

"After what 50 Cent's been through—shot nine times, overcoming street life—there are lots of worse things that he could be doing than lip-syncing," Dooley said of the rapper.

Boyd, on the other hand, had an old-fashioned preference when it came to performing. He couldn't believe how many of the newer artists resorted to lip-sync.

"How could you possibly know if they're lip-syncing?" Kevin asked Boyd doubtfully.

"I just read their lips," he replied.

Reading lips: genius!

Kevin believed that learning to read lips would solve a problem he was having when wearing the earplugs: he couldn't understand what anyone was saying. Boyd said he knew of a music coach who taught lip-sync. He even arranged for her to visit the funeral home for a couple of hours. She helped Kevin understand specific movements that the mouth, jaw, and cheeks make for certain sounds. Kevin felt like he'd discovered the keys to the universe, and that if he could just master lip reading he could return to a normal, dance-free life.

By the time Martino had died, Kevin had not only had the visit from the lip-sync coach, but he had also spent two days watching lip-reading instructional videos while practicing on Boyd, Missy, Dooley, Dotty, and Barry. It became sort of a game in which someone would say something to Kevin while he was wearing the plugs and he would have to repeat what they said. If he got it right, the person would nod "yes," if not, then the person would shake his or her head "no."

In the middle of one of these practice sessions with Dooley, Kevin had an unexpected visit from Amy. He decided to try his new, developing skill on her, only this time, instead of Amy—who wasn't aware of Kevin's illness—nodding or shaking her head, Dooley stood near her and discreetly signaled to Kevin if he was making any sense. This would be a real-world test run. Kevin wanted to keep his bizarre illness a secret, known to as few people as possible. He certainly did not want Amy, of all people, to learn of his freakish condition.

Missy sent Amy to Kevin's office. She looked breathtaking as usual, today in a simple pair of jeans and a very ordinary white blouse. The first few sentences were easy enough.

"Hi," she began,

Kevin replied, "Hi, how are you?"

Dooley nodded.

"Okay. It's going to take some time," she answered.

"I know. There's nothing I can say."

Dooley gave him a thumbs-up.

"Well, I just wanted to drop the payment off and say thanks for everything," she continued.

Kevin didn't know what she was saying, but because she placed a check on his desk, he knew it had something to do with the payment.

"Oh, thank you. You were happy with everything?"

Dooley nodded, simultaneously giving him a 'thumbs-up.'

Amy seemed to notice that there was something going on between the two of them. She looked from Dooley, who immediately tucked his hands into his pockets, to Kevin.

"Yes," she answered, "Your company did a great job."

"Good, good. The headstone should be ready in about two weeks."

"Great. Thanks again."

Suddenly she became nervous, glancing towards Dooley's direction, then to her feet, then shifting her eyes briefly to Kevin and back to the floor. The lip reading started to get a little more challenging.

"Umm, there was something else, too," she said.

Kevin had no idea what she was saying, because she appeared to be speaking to the floor. He shrugged his shoulders and looked towards Dooley for help. Dooley raised his eyebrows and grimaced, unsure of what to do.

"I'm sorry?" Kevin asked.

She looked at him, then to Dooley, then back towards Kevin. She was uncomfortable about something.

"Umm, I was just wondering, as long as this isn't too inappropriate…"

Kevin was lost, staring at Dooley for help.

"What did you say? You were 'once under a long ancient trooper reader'?"

She was dumbfounded. Dooley shook his head emphatically, 'No.'

She laughed. "What? That's not what I said at all. I'm sorry, I don't know why I'm so nervous."

Boyd suddenly bounced into the office, oblivious to the charade.

"Hey, dancing fool!" he greeted Kevin, "How's that lip-rrr…" He halted himself, noticing Amy. Dooley and Kevin both shook their heads at Boyd. Boyd looked at one of Kevin's ears, noticing the earplug, and promptly became keen to the game.

"Ahhmm… I was saying… How's that lipstick coming along?" he said, covering himself. "You know, the new one I ordered for that new body?" He looked at Amy, but asked Kevin again, slowly, carefully enunciating each sound, "The lll…ipppp..sssti...ckkk."

"Oh, yeah, that lipstick," Kevin answered, "Uhhh…I already put it in your room."

"Thanks, thanks," Boyd said. "I'll be off then. Well, it's nice to see you, Amy. I know the circumstances aren't the best, but your mother was a lovely woman, and I can see much of her passion for life in you. I told Kevin here he should give you a call, but he's a shy one. You'd think after all his years in this business, that by now he'd have more of an appreciation for how short life is."

He winked at her, laughed, and left the room.

Kevin had absolutely no idea what Boyd said after "Thanks, thanks." He shrugged his shoulders towards Dooley, who shrugged his shoulders in return.

"Well, would you, then, Kevin?" she asked him, "That's what I wanted to ask."

Dooley nodded his head, vigorously.

"What?" Kevin asked, then realizing that Dooley was trying to signal him to say "yes," he told her, "Yes, yes, sure. Yes, yes. Definitely. We can take care of that right away."

"Great," she smiled and turned to leave the room. "I wasn't sure if you had some kind of policy about dating clients or anything."

"No, I think Esther's shoes will be safe in the casket. You won't need the police for that."

Her face crumpled as she gave him a baffled gaze. Dooley shook his head, and then tried to cover Kevin's mistake by covering it with laughter.

"Kevin, you crack me up!" Dooley remarked.

Amy formed a half-hearted but confused smile, said, "Well, you have my number," and turned towards the doorway.

"Okay," Kevin said, not sure if she was leaving or going to use the restroom.

"Bye," she said and waved.

"Bye."

After Amy left the home, Dooley explained what she was asking, and to what Kevin had agreed. Kevin thought for sure that Dooley was playing a prank on him. The idea that someone like Amy Best would ever ask someone like Kevin McCormick to call her was ridiculous. It came down to a handshake bet between Dooley and Kevin before Kevin agreed to call Amy: if Dooley was wrong, he would have to dance by himself at a time, place, and to a song of Kevin's choosing, but if he was right, Kevin would be doing the dancing.

"You promise to keep your word?" Dooley asked.

"Yeah, yeah," Kevin assured him, confident that Dooley must have misinterpreted something Amy had said. "When have you known me to ever welsh on a bet?"

*   *   *

"La Bohème. It's an opera by Giacomo Puccini. It's an Italian opera, but it's loosely based on French bohemian…poor…lifestyle. It's a love story. La bohème is the main female character," Boyd explained to Kevin, who had just entered the embalming room while Boyd was preparing Martino's body. Kevin was curious about what he was hearing from Boyd's stereo.

"You seem to be handling it okay," Boyd noted.

"It's not so bad," Kevin answered, swaying to the strings and wind instruments.

"How's he coming along?" he asked. They only had a few more hours before the open-casket wake.

"He'll be ready," Boyd assured him.

Martino was a rare case for the McCormick Funeral Home; they didn't perform many traditional Italian services. There were numerous Italian funeral home competitors spread out across the neighboring towns, and it was typical that most Italians preferred to make their funeral arrangements with them. Although Harry had many friends in the Italian community, the McCormick Home had hosted only a few of these over the years, each time under unusual circumstances.

The Martino family was very traditional. Antonio and Gina had made many trips to Italy over the years to visit relatives, so this one baffled Kevin when he first took the call. However, Boyd later explained the history to him: Mr. Martino fought alongside Kevin's grandfather, Gavin McCormick, during World War II. Once they realized that they were from neighboring towns, they agreed to look each other up after the war. It wasn't until a couple of years after the war that they had caught up with one another. Antonio was struggling to get his masonry business off the ground, while Gavin, a carpenter, was making strides in his casket-making business and was getting ready to expand into offering more funeral services. He had an idea for a "one-stop-shop" funeral center, and had a couple of other war veteran buddies who were skilled florists and candlemakers. He offered Antonio the project of constructing the building for this center, which eventually became the McCormick Funeral Home: the very same structure that Kevin was operating today.

"I had heard about him, but I never met him, until today," Boyd said, pointing his chin towards Antonio's corpse. "You know, that Don character told me something he had heard him say only a few days ago: that this home here was his first real project. Got his whole business started right here. He was proud of it, and forever grateful to Gavin for giving him his chance. Antonio told Don that he drove by this place hundreds of times, and always felt that it was part of him."

"Yeah, but I don't get it," Kevin commented, "That was so long ago. This guy owns half of Saugus. He's got to be one of the wealthiest people around. My grandfather's been dead for over fifteen years, and this isn't exactly a premiere establishment. I mean, our most expensive casket costs less than four grand."

"Lots of people wouldn't understand," lectured Boyd, "That kind of loyalty is very rare these days. It's a value that isn't emphasized as much in this cut-throat world today, but it's a sort of awakening that a lot of folks develop when they get older and start reflecting on their lives, and the people who helped them out along the way.

"Life isn't about titles or trophies or how many lands you've conquered, how enemies you've vanquished, how many toys you've collected. It's about relationships: what you've put into them, what you get out of them. That's it. The nature of your relationships determines what you get out of life, what everything means to you."

"Thanks for the tip, Boyd, but right now life is about Mr. Martino being ready for his viewing. Otherwise, Don and Sal will see to it that I don't get much more out of life at all."

TEN

As Kevin inspected the home's appearance for the Martino wake, he thought about how different it would be from his own family's wakes and from the types of wakes his home typically arranged. He thought about wakes in general, wondering if he would ever want one for himself. He had been taught that viewings were primarily a Christian practice, tracing to hundreds of years ago, when medical technology wasn't always one hundred percent certain that a person might actually be dead. The body would be presented in a viewing state for a day or two to see if it would "awaken."

He understood how quickly bodies begin to deteriorate upon death. He imagined that centuries ago, these wakes may have carried on far too long perhaps due to family members in denial. He had seen how the body tends to move on its own during the deterioration process, as muscles tighten, fluids shift, and organs weaken, and he had heard tales of people insisting that the deceased was trying to "wake up" when in reality it was most likely the body beginning to rot. In some cultures, he knew, the body must be buried within twenty-four hours of death.

At his own family's funerals, there was always lots of drinking, laughing, and telling jokes about the deceased. The jokes often included tales about all the stupid and silly things for which the person was remembered: "I recall that evenin' when Tommy and I had so much whisky we fell asleep in the snow and woke the next morn' in frozen dog piss... or maybe it was our own piss... I can't remember," was a fairly typical story, followed by roaring laughter.

Much of those stories were exaggerated as well, at times completely fictitious. In fact, Kevin had heard some of the same exact stories told for several different people.

At Harry's wake, Kevin was struck by how many people described his father as one of their closest friends. One person after another approached Kevin with a comment such as "he was one of the most genuine people you'd ever meet" or "one of the few people you could truly trust" or "you always knew where you stood with Harry."

After the wake, as was typical in many Irish circles around Boston, Harry's closest friends capped the evening with a few drinks at one of his favorite pubs. In Malden, it was O'Neill's: a sports bar that had live music a few nights a week in the downtown area known as Malden Square. That night at O'Neill's, some of the more private legends of Harry were told, including war, high school, romantic, and sports stories. There was one story in particular of which Harry never spoke but Kevin had heard bits and pieces over the years. Harry would always order whoever was referencing the tale to "be quiet" and he would dismiss it as "nonsense."

At Harry's post-wake gathering at O'Neill's, it was the first time Kevin had heard this legend in its entirety.

"It was before they were married," Harry's longtime friend, Chris O'Connor, began.

O'Connor was a tall, scrawny man who played professional minor league hockey in the early seventies. He had a reputation as an "enforcer": a tough guy carried on hockey benches exclusively to produce consequences if the other team decided to get too far out of hand. His talent to mix it up earned him two very brief stints with the parent club. Things didn't go quite as well as O'Connor hoped; in each altercation, he left the ice on a stretcher. Still, he was entrenched in the team's folklore especially because he was a local boy. He was also embraced by the fans who adored anyone who stepped into the ring to protect their more beloved hockey icons. After his underachieving hockey stint, O'Connor excelled in a second career, which was aligned with his second passion: selling liquor.

"Dotty was a waitress at the old Summer Street Diner," O'Connor said, flipped a shot of Black Label down his throat, and continued, "They were datin'.

"There was this police officer, Mickey Roy, who liked to throw his badge in people's faces. Everybody hated him. He'd bust people for no reason, and then force 'em to do stuff or give him stuff to avoid being taken in: money, food, jewelry…a variety of other despicable shit you might classify as… 'forced favors'… and whatever else he could come up with. In those days there were lots of corrupt cops around here, but this guy was the worst. You should have seen how places would clear out whenever he stepped foot into them. It was like, 'Hey, here comes Mickey,' and everyone would scatter like mice. He was a pure asshole.

"Anyway, Mickey had a thing for Dotty while she was datin' Harry. He was always hittin' on her, with his asshole grin, stoppin' by the diner for coffee whenever she was workin', always hangin' around too long, grabbin' her body, tryin' to grope her and sayin'… graphic… stuff… to her. These were the days long before you could do much about sexual harassment, especially when it involved a dirty cop. Dotty never said anythin'. She knew Harry would explode if he ever found out, and she didn't want him to get into any trouble.

"But you've got to understand how much everybody hated Mickey, and how sick we all were of the corruption downtown.

"Eventually the word got back to Harry. The rumor is that one of Mickey's enemies on the force told Harry about it. So Harry goes to the coffee shop one day. Waits for Mickey. Dotty's workin'. She tells Harry he should probably get goin' before the next wave—which would include Mickey on his shift—came through the joint. She says somethin' about how it's gonna get real busy and she won't have time to talk to him anyway. Harry assures her that all he wanted to do was say 'hi' to an old friend of his and then he'd be on his way.

"So Mickey shows up. Laughs when he sees Harry waitin' for him there. Harry offers to buy him a coffee. Mickey says he's all set: he gets his for free. Harry offers to pour it for him. Mickey obliges. Holdin' the pot, Harry asks Mickey if he ever heard of Jack Sleeper."

O'Connor turned to Kevin, "You ever hear of him?"

Kevin shook his head 'no.'

"Jack Sleeper, accordin' to your dad, and accordin' to what he told Mickey Roy, was a phantom, or a ghost, or some psycho on the loose around Malden. Nobody knew for sure. Nobody's ever actually seen him. The legend was that Sleeper was killed by some corrupt cops who were after a stash of cash in his family's house over on Dexter Street, in the older part of town, decades ago. At that time, some people said it happened maybe fifty or sixty years earlier.

"Well, as your dad explained to Mickey, every few years since, Sleeper resurfaces, mysteriously, and some local dirty cop disappears. Sometimes from Malden, sometimes from a neighboring town."

"It's true," another of Harry's old friends—a cop— interrupted, explaining to Kevin, "If you check the records of the towns around here, it's really weird; at least once every ten years, some cop mysteriously vanishes. Usually somebody who was involved in something dirty. Sometimes right from their cruisers, a couple of other times guys just disappeared on their way home after their shifts, never to be seen again. All of the disappearances are still unexplained."

"That's right," O'Connor resumed the story, "And when Harry was done tellin' Mickey about the legend of Sleeper, he very slowly, carefully, poured Mickey another cup of coffee. He tells him that he's also heard Sleeper really hates dirtbags who disrespect women.

"Now, Harry's family had been livin' in Malden for close to eighty years at that time, so the story had to have some legitimacy to it, at least to a dumbass like Mickey.

"Harry hands Mickey his coffee. As Mickey drinks, it, Harry tells him that people had their ideas about how Sleeper works: some say he follows them home after a dirty shift, some say he sets up what seems like an innocent police call, like a broken-down vehicle in some alley late at night, only to ambush the cop, some say he gradually poisons the cops' drinks when he visit places like…local coffee shops.

"Harry winks at Mickey and tells him to drink up.

"Then, your dad, Harry, tells Mickey one last thing. He says, 'You know Mickey, my older relatives who knew about Sleeper would say that he had this creepy reputation for appearing out of the blue in trees, bushes, and windows. Appearin' all of a sudden and then disappearin' just as quick into the shadows. Even before Sleeper died or became this phantom or whatever happened to him, he had this creepy quality already.'

"Mickey tells Harry to shut the hell up and get out of 'his' diner.

"So Harry tells Mickey to enjoy his coffee and leaves.

"Nobody really knows what exactly happened to Mickey over the next couple of weeks after that conversation. Some people say that Harry followed him into an alley one night, threw a sack over him, and beat the piss out of him. I've heard that Harry left a skunk in the backseat of Mickey's cruiser another night. Another story was that Harry slipped a sleepin' pill or somethin' into Mickey's coffee that day, and the next mornin' some people found Mickey buried up to his neck, still in his uniform, at Revere beach, cryin' his ass off like a little girl. When they pulled him out of the sand, he was handcuffed and had pissed and crapped himself. Mickey's neighbors said that on nights he wasn't workin', he'd leave every single light on in his entire house, all night long. Dotty claims she never saw him drink anythin' from that coffee shop ever again, and after a week never showed his face in that place neither.

"Harry's story, as you know Kev', is that he never did anythin'. But we all know Harry! And, if you ask me, and few people knew Harry like I did, there is some truth to all of the above."

The group cheered and toasted Kevin's father.

"At any rate," O'Connor continued after gulping another swig of the scotch-whisky mix, "the best part of the story is that Mickey stopped botherin' people. And a lot of the corruption downtown stopped, too."

Antonio Martino would certainly have his share of these stories told today. But his wake would be very different from Harry's despite how close their friendship was. Kevin planned to stay in hiding as much as possible during Martino's wake. Traditional Italian wakes had always made Kevin a little uncomfortable. It wasn't because of the music. In fact, this wake would not include any music at all. Nor was it because of the scent from hundreds of candles that would be filling the home. Rather, it was because after he witnessed the atmosphere at the Martino house, he knew that this was going to be a classic return-to-roots Sicilian service. There would be crying, lots of crying, and then even more crying. And in between that: a torrential downpour of…crying. He had seen this before; it would be a competition to see who could cry the most and loudest. Many people would be crying, incredibly, without managing to shed a single tear.

Accompanying the Crying Olympics would also be an outpouring of stories—legends —that exalted the dead person to superhuman status. These over-embellished stories often resulted in excessive hugging and kissing.

Nevertheless, some of the myths that Kevin had heard in the "Glorious Tale" challenge were impressive and would even put some Bible legends to shame. For example, at another Sicilian wake years ago, a woman who nobody apparently recognized shouted that the deceased landscaper had once "single-handedly saved my entire family," tears streaming, hands raised as if praising a god, "from a deadly swarm of killer bees! With only one of his own shoes to protect himself!"

Kevin had met some very superstitious Italians at these events in the past. It was an odd thing: for two or three days people would bawl until they could barely speak, sometimes exhausting themselves to the point at which they would faint. But once the casket had been lowered into the ground, those same people would never speak of that deceased person ever again. A wise, elderly woman once explained to him that talking about the dead would encourage them to stick around for a while.

He tried talking about his dad, a lot, after Harry had died, hoping desperately to keep him around. It didn't work.

So it wasn't the music that he was avoiding this time. Instead, it was because the traditional Sicilian grieving process as he had seen it in these situations was about as polar opposite from his own Irish-Scottish roots as he could get.

Mercifully, Antonio Martino's wake was on a weeknight evening at seven o'clock and lasted only three hours, remarkably brief for a man who was such a pillar in his community. Other than stopping by the viewing room every so often to make sure that nothing had caught fire due to all of the candles, to see if someone had fainted, or to refill the tissue boxes, Kevin sat in his office for nearly the entire service.

*   *   *

At the start of Martino's funeral, Kevin was confident that not only had he and Dooley worked out the kinks since the debacle at Esther Best's funeral, but also that he would be capably soundproofed from the addition of earplugs and his newfound lip-reading skill. This time, they even went so far as to ask the church choir to rehearse before the funeral, so that Kevin could test the earplugs. They explained that the family was particular about the style of music. As the choir rehearsed, Kevin and Dooley would ask them to reduce the volume depending on how much Kevin could hear through the earplugs. They hid Kevin's problem simply by lying that there would be some guests at the funeral with extremely sensitive ears. Eventually, they managed to reach a balance that he could tolerate.

The strategy worked incredibly well, at first. He had waited until moments before the Mass started to tuck the plugs into his ears. No one seemed to notice. The casket rolled in as the choir sang "The Strife is O'er." Kevin could barely hear that or the painful howling, wailing, and shrieking of many of the mourners, dressed in a sea of black clothing. The music still got to him a little bit, but he just kept trying to move, shifting his feet, hands, and adjusting his tie: whatever he could do to hide the otherwise obvious impact that the sounds were having over him.

For the most part, not being able to hear very well wasn't a big deal. Kevin had directed hundreds of these services over the years, many of those with Dooley and Barry, so the three of them could get it done together with little conversation at all. Also, both Dooley and Barry were aware of Kevin's earplugs, so they did their best to cover for him if someone was trying to get his attention and he didn't hear them. In general, people don't talk much during funerals anyway, so perfect hearing was not critical. And if people did have something to say, it was usually predictable, such as "Where am I supposed to sit?" or "Do we go now?" so Kevin felt that his lip-reading would be more than adequate to tie up any loose ends.

There were a couple of glitches, however. The first occurred as the pallbearers assembled in the church foyer. The space was crowded, as Mr. Martino not only had a very large family, but also had many fellow war veterans who wanted to be part of his procession. Kevin asked that all but military personnel remove their hats before the entrance procession began. One of the men standing near Kevin dropped his hat altogether in the process, right near Kevin's feet.

Given the crowded space and an awkward angle, the man could not reach his hat and instead asked Kevin, "Can you please pick my hat up?"

Kevin heard his muffled voice, but interpreted his lips as saying it as "Can you please give me a hug?"

It wasn't often that people at these events asked the funeral director for a hug, especially men, but Kevin had seen a broad range of odd requests over the years. This was a minor request, so he took a step towards the man and embraced him. The man returned the exchange, seizing Kevin with a mighty bear-hug, and exploded into streaming tears and loud moans. Everyone in the foyer froze, acknowledging the spectacle. From the corner of his eye, Kevin saw Dooley pick up the man's hat and hand it to him.

Dooley glared at Kevin and mouthed "What are you doing?!"

Kevin would later learn that the man he hugged was Antonio's only brother, Angelo. They were as close as siblings could get, even fighting alongside each other at one point in World War II. Angelo, however, fell into a downward spiral of alcoholism after losing his wife to cancer eighteen years before. When Antonio became gravely ill, he asked Angelo to sober up before he died.

At the time of the funeral, Angelo had finally been completely sober for three weeks.

Angelo could not calm himself, so they had to proceed walking the casket down the center aisle with Angelo clinging to the side of the casket, in so much grief that he could barely walk. He fell down twice during the procession, each time pallbearers abandoning the casket to help him back to his feet. The casket was perched on a rolling cart, so it was never in danger of falling.

Don and Sal scowled at Kevin during this entire procession.

Eventually, the casket made it to the front of the church and Angelo was helped to his seat, where his moans weren't as noticeable because they blended in with the rest of the emphatic crying. The service resumed a normal course, and Kevin hoped Don and Sal had forgotten about the earlier episode with Angelo. Kevin tried his best to remain inconspicuous, but his restless body continually caught Don's attention. At one point, Don tapped Sal on the shoulder, making sure that Sal saw how Kevin's body shook and shivered whenever music played. They each gave Kevin a puzzled evil eye. All of Kevin's preparation for this funeral was not quite enough to hide his problem. In the middle of the funeral, it was too late for him to try and sneak out. If he could only hang on until the end of the Mass, he'd probably be okay, since there would only be a bugle playing "Taps" at the graveside service.

Unfortunately, he wouldn't get the chance to hang on.

Gina Martino didn't walk very well, and even with the walker she needed assistance. A younger woman, the same one that Kevin had seen a few days earlier at the Martino home, had helped Gina throughout the entire funeral, including communion, the part of the Catholic Mass in which certain participants approach a priest or other designated person to receive the eucharist. Usually this involves walking down the church's main aisle, then around the pews to the opposite side, and back into one's own pew, all in a circular route that leads back to one's original seat.

As communion began, the choir broke into the hymn "Be Not Afraid," a steady, slow song, usually vocally heavy and with lots of long notes.

Gina sat in the first pew, draped head-to-toe in charcoal black, her entire face shielded by a dark veil. When communion began, she could have easily sat in the handicapped area and thus not been subjected to any walking at all. However, for some reason she insisted on following the traditional pattern. This surprised Kevin, who thought for sure she was simply going to remain in the handicapped area. Kevin walked towards her and politely informed her that walking the whole route would not be necessary. She responded with something in Italian, but Kevin had not yet started reading lips in any foreign language. He looked towards the younger woman for an explanation, but she immediately broke down, sobbing. As the three of them stood in the middle of the walkway in front of the pews, Don approached them to sort out the confusion.

Don spoke to the younger, sobbing woman first. He nodded to her, stepped back, and said to Kevin, "Please step towards the plants," referring to the numerous bouquets that were lining the side of the walkway closest to the altar.

"What?" Kevin asked, unable to clearly see Don's mouth.

"Please—step—towards   the   plants!"   Don enunciated, annoyed.

What Kevin interpreted, however, was "Please—zip—up your pants!" Shaken with embarrassment, he immediately looked towards the zipper in the front of his pants and promptly examined it.

Seems perfectly closed to me.

He tugged on it, hastily trying to remain discreet, to make sure he wasn't missing something. When he raised his head so that his eyes met Don's, he realized in one instant that not only had he gotten the lipreading interpretation incorrect, but also that he had grotesquely offended Don with what *Don* had interpreted as a rude gesture towards him.

With one of his huge hands, Don forcefully thumped his palm against Kevin's chest. The violent shove moved Kevin out of the way of Gina and her female assistant. It also knocked out one of his earplugs, projecting it somewhere into the dozens of bouquets. There was no way he was going to find it. The spares were conveniently out in the hearse's glove compartment. His head began to ring with panic. He decided that running out on Martino's funeral would have much more bearable consequences than sticking around to perform whatever his body was about to do. He started, as calmly as possible, towards the nearest exit.

The calm lasted about four steps.

The lead choir singer's voice cracked through Kevin's skull as if he were struck by a bullet. It felt like a knife had torn through his spine. He thought his ears were going to burst. His entire body quaked.

Suddenly, everything settled for a few seconds. He noticed the entire congregation, except for the choir, anxiously watching him as the seizure took hold. This time, it was a flighty dance: he leaped in short bursts, as much as an overweight, out-of-shape, thirty-seven-year-old man with no dancing training could leap. He pushed off one leg, landing on the other, alternating directions. Lightly waving his arms as if conducting an orchestra, his body added a couple of slow spins here and there to enhance the leaping.

The priest wasn't sure what to do, but Don and Sal were. They each seized one of Kevin's arms and dragged his wriggling body down the aisle along one of the walls, all the way towards the back of the church, throwing him into an enclosed confessional booth. Sal stood outside the booth while Don stepped inside and closed the door.

The beating wasn't as bad as Kevin had anticipated. The first punch to his midsection knocked the wind out him. He swore that Don tried to break one of his legs, but it would not stop moving, so he couldn't land a solid blow to it. The most devastating strike was an elbow to the nose, which left Kevin dazed and bleeding. There were a few more punches to his stomach, before Don picked him up and dropped him against the wall. The final blow was a direct hit to Kevin's jaw.

Incredibly, and to Don's frustrated dismay, Kevin continued to dance throughout the entire beating.

Nevertheless, when he was satisfied that Kevin had gotten the message, he took the keys to the hearse from Kevin's pocket. "We're taking it from here," he declared, then concluded with a finger in Kevin's bloodied face, "The church is a holy place! Don't bring your disrespectful filth in here!"

He left the room and slammed the door behind him as the music ended. Within seconds, Dooley and Barry arrived to see if he was okay.

"Kev, you're bleeding," Dooley so helpfully observed.

"Thanks Dooley. I could have figured that out myself."

"Are you okay?" Barry asked.

"Yeah, I'll be okay. They've got the keys to the hearse. Follow them to the grave and get the hearse back when they're done with it."

Kevin slumped back into the confessional booth as Dooley and Barry returned to the service. There he remained, surviving the final, recessional hymn as the mourners filed out of the church. Happy to be alive, he rested in the booth, enjoying the quiet solitude.

His solace was broken when Father Walsh, a priest who he had known for years and with whom he had conducted many funerals, opened the door.

"Jesus, Kevin! What are you doing in here?" Walsh asked him. "You're bleeding everywhere! I just got a call from Dooley. He says he's been trying to get a hold of you. Says the last they saw of you, you were getting your head bashed in by a couple of mafia goons."

"Yeah, Father, that about sums it up."

"What is going on with you?" Father Walsh asked him, helping him to his feet. "I heard that you were dancing around in the middle of the Martino funeral today? Is that true?"

"Yes, that is correct."

"And I also heard that you vandalized—destroyed— a one-hundred-year-old vase at the Best funeral a few days ago?"

"Correct."

"Well then, what's the matter?" Walsh asked with an air of angry concern.

Kevin was at a loss. He'd been to several doctors already. He'd even seen a therapist. No one could help him or even tell him what was wrong.

"Father, have you ever performed an exorcism?" He figured that it wouldn't hurt: he'd tried everything else.

"An exorcism? You think you're possessed?"

"Nobody's been able to figure out what's wrong with me, so I think it might be a possibility."

"A demon spirit has taken residence inside your body?"

"More or less, yes."

"You watch too many movies, Kevin. What is this demon doing to you?"

"It's making me dance."

"Making you dance?"

"Yes. Out of control. Every time I hear music, I have to dance, against my will. It makes me do all these spins and leaps and twists and all this crazy stuff. I don't know how to stop it. I've tried medication and earplugs. There's no way to stop it."

"Oh yes, I know this one," Walsh said with a trace of sarcasm.

"You do?"

"Yes, the old 'Dancing Demon': jumps into people's bodies, makes them dance like freaks."

"Seriously? Can you get it out of me? How hard is it to do?"

"Pretty easy, actually. I can do it right now, in fact."

Kevin sighed, thankfully relieved. "Please get rid of it, if you can," he begged.

With an open hand, Walsh smacked Kevin across his bloodied face.

"Oww, Father, what was that?"

"The power of Christ compels you!" Walsh shouted, mocking Kevin.

It took Kevin a moment before he realized that Walsh was toying with him.

"The power of Christ compels you!" Walsh repeated, whacking Kevin across the face once again.

"Oww! Okay, Father, I get it," Kevin said, raising his arms to protect himself against another blow. "I'm not possessed."

"No, you're not possessed," Walsh concluded, "You're just being an ass. Now get this problem of yours straightened out," he said walking away, "and don't bring your reckless, disrespectful antics in here ever again! This is the house of God! Asshole!"

When Dooley and Barry finally arrived to take him home, Dooley expressed pleasant surprise at how well Don and Sal had directed the remainder of the service.

"Don had a no-nonsense style, and everyone followed his instructions perfectly," he explained. "It was amazing how smoothly things went, like they were in the funeral business themselves or something."

"So we asked him," Barry said, "If they'd ever worked for a funeral home before. He looked at me with this stone-dead face and said 'Yeah, sure. We have a clean and efficient burial service of our own.'"

ELEVEN

Kevin called fifty-three restaurants before finding Cantina Siesta, a Mexican restaurant about one block from the ocean waterfront strip in Newburyport, Massachusetts. It was an hour from Malden, but only forty minutes from Amy's condo in Andover. Each of the first fifty-two restaurants answered "yes" to Kevin's question about whether or not they played dining music. Cantina Siesta *did* play dining music, but it was limited to the indoor seating area. However, the restaurant also had an outdoor patio that was music-free. It did not take reservations, but Kevin insisted on making one.

"We are just a walk-in pub. I have been here five years and never booked a reservation," a hostess told Kevin over the phone.

"You don't understand," Kevin explained, "We'll be driving a long way, and it's sort of a handicapped thing with certain sounds."

The hostess, who was also apparently a bartender and waitress for the pub, finally relented and promised him a table for two at seven that evening.

Kevin and Amy arranged to meet at the restaurant. They would take their own cars. Kevin had never heard of Cantina Siesta, so he figured he'd arrive very early, to make sure there were no surprises. He had two sets of earplugs in his pocket, just in case.

When Kevin arrived at the restaurant, he understood immediately why they didn't need to take reservations. The front of Cantina Seista had a prime view of the parking lot across the street. The rear of the restaurant had a view of the backs of three- and four-story buildings, some perhaps a century old. This exterior patio bordered an L-shaped road that wrapped around it, leading from the parking lot at the front. Kevin could see that the road served as a convenient cut-through to the waterfront area for people whose cars were parked in that lot. This part of the restaurant only had six tables, surrounded by a three-foot-high fence, perhaps to prevent people from skipping out to the waterfront before paying their tabs.

Kevin was glad that he had reserved the table outside by the cut-through street, with the view of the fence and backs of buildings, because the inside of the restaurant reeked of beer and liquor, the dank stench permeating the floor, walls, tables, and chairs. It was dark inside, very dimly lit, perhaps to keep people from noticing the gnats, cockroaches, food stains, and rodents. The bar was decorated by some tacky Christmas lights, lining the front of the bar, above it, and wrapped around the bar posts. No doubt, they were placed intentionally to help drunks find their way to the restroom.

Just follow the trail of lights around the corner.

The sticky floor clung to the soles of his shoes as he entered the restaurant. The air smelled of stale, burned frialator grease. When he introduced himself to the hostess behind the bar, a cook/dishwasher/busboy covered in a filthy uniform brushed by him with a bucket full of dirty dishes. Through a window that provided a view into the kitchen, he noticed a gum-chewing waitress adjust her hair before she grabbed the plates for a party. One of the cooks standing across from her was sweating a storm that was undoubtedly raining into whatever he was cooking.

Kevin wore his earplugs through the inside of the restaurant as the hostess led him across the liquor-plastered floor to the patio outside. He took his seat at the table she had reserved for him: the only table in the entire restaurant with a tablecloth. Actually, it looked more like an old cooking apron, but the ties had been cut from it. The table was also candlelit, by a birthday candle jammed

109

into what appeared to be a wad of gum in a shot-glass. Kevin wondered if the chunk of gum was perhaps something the waitress he noticed through the kitchen window had put together.

He asked the hostess to please make sure that the sliding doors that led to the patio remained closed, since his ears were extremely sensitive to certain pitches of music. She assured him that it wouldn't be a problem, explaining that they rarely have any customers who want to sit outside at night in late September.

Seated at his birthday-candle-lit table next to the rotting fence, Kevin removed his earplugs. Except for some traffic noise on some nearby streets and voices from people cutting through on their way to the waterfront, it was beautifully quiet. His choice of venue couldn't have been much better.

Perfect!

Amy also arrived much earlier than expected.

"I wasn't sure where this place was," she explained as she sat at the table and examined the bottoms of her pumps. "I just wanted to make sure I wasn't too late. How did you hear about this place?"

"Oh, a friend suggested it," he lied, "He said it was nice and quiet and a short walk to the waterfront."

"Yeah," she commented, looking puzzled, "Strange how quiet it is out back here though. I mean, the only sounds here at all are the traffic around the corner."

"Nice for a change, isn't it?"

"Sure," she said, politely. "I thought you picked this place because of the mariachi band."

He froze. "The what?"

"The mariachi band. They start at six-thirty. That's when you told me to be here." She smiled, brandishing her perfect white teeth.

"Mariachi band?" He was unaware of this. He looked around frantically for signs of the band. He hadn't noticed anything when he walked into the place.

"Oh, come on, I've seen how much you love music. You can't pull a fast one on me: I knew you'd pick a place with great music."

"Well, actually…"

"I told them to make sure they include us when they make their rounds."

"Yeah, well, you know, I've been listening to so much music lately that I thought it would be nice for a change to take a break from it."

"Oh, just one song." She motioned toward the restaurant door, waving someone towards them.

Kevin was mortified as he noticed the mariachi band almost magically materialize from inside the restaurant. They acknowledged Amy's gesturing and gathered their instruments.

"No, really Amy, we don't have to do that," he nervously feigned a laugh.

"Sure we do. Come on, how often do you get these opportunities. It'll be fun!"

The band opened the glass sliding doors, invading Kevin's sanctuary.

"Maybe, but a nice quiet talk can be fun too," he said as the band drew closer to their table.

"Oh, just one song, please."

"Hey, maybe we should find another restaurant."

"Kevin…"

"Hey, you know what, I have to go to the bathroom, badly," Kevin said as he started to rise from the table.

"Don't be silly," she laughed, "Let's just hear them. Come on, it won't hurt."

I'm not so sure about that.

The band had three members: one heavyset man carrying a large, bass guitarrón, a handsome, thin, dark-haired man, no doubt the lead mariachi who also played the more rhythmic vihuela guitar, and a short, gray-haired male trumpet player. Reaching for his earplugs at that moment would have been incredibly rude and resulted in a lot of undesirable explaining. And with all three members of the mariachi band plus Amy staring at him, there was no way he could retrieve them from his pocket discreetly. He could only hope that their first song was something very quiet.

"Madam," the dark-haired man with the vihuela began, "Do you have a request?"

"Yes, yes, I do," Kevin interjected, "How about a very, very soft version of 'Twinkle Twinkle Little Star,' with no instruments?"

The mariachi musicians gave him a brief, blank stare, trying to figure out if he was serious, before the elder trumpet-player laughed.

"You're funny," Amy remarked, tapping Kevin on the shoulder. "Let's hear some real mariachi. How about 'La Cucaracha'?"

Otherwise known as "Doom," Kevin thought. He braced himself, wrapping his legs as best as he could around the legs of his chair, closing his eyes, his hands gripping the armrests for dear life. The trumpet began, tearing through the September night air, bouncing from the ground, the walls, the windows in the alley: prrrrummpp ep ep prumpitty pep pep prrr prr prr prepp…. The guitarrón joined in, providing a steady background bass: thump thump thump thummpty thump thump. Kevin could feel the blood pulsing in his legs, matching the beat of the guitarrón. They weren't even ten seconds into the song, but he could already feel it working its way steadily up his spine, then across his shoulders, down into his elbows. He clenched his teeth and tried desperately to think of something other than what he was hearing.

> *"La cucaracha, la cucaracha,*
> *ya no puede caminar,*
> *porque no tiene, porque le falta,*
> *las dos patitas de atrás…"*

Kevin didn't know much about mariachi, but at that very moment he learned the hard way that peppering trumpet notes can probably lead to brain damage, reverberating through his skull like boulders bouncing around in an empty steel dumpster.

That was the easy part.

When the mariachi's voice rolled into the second verse—the melody trapped in the alley—his fingers drifting across the vihuela, it was all Kevin could take. His body ripped out of his grip to join the fast-paced notes. His legs marched rapidly in random directions, somewhat along with the trumpet. He had no prior notion that his muscles were capable of moving so quickly. His shoulders, arms, and neck seemed to be more preoccupied with the main melody, rolling and rotating up and down, side-to-side.

The worst part of this was that Kevin's behavior only encouraged the band to play even louder. Apparently they mistook his seizure as enthusiasm. His movements became more emphatic as the decibels increased. During one lurch-and-spin, he knocked over a table and some chairs. Two of the other restaurant staff members, who had apparently noticed the action, ran to move those furniture pieces to safety along with some other items that might be in danger of his relentless path of destruction. Effectively, they had created a private dance floor for Kevin on the patio.

His body exploited it. His hippity-hopping opened up, adding some side-to-side leaps and at one point even sent him into a somersault. At another point, he bit his tongue.

By the time the song had finished, the entire restaurant staff and all of the patrons from inside the restaurant had stepped out onto the patio to watch Kevin's—and the mariachi band's—performance. The singer ended the song by holding an excessively long and passionate note, which was simultaneously played by the trumpet and enhanced by the fast-paced-repetitive strumming of both the vihuela and guitarrón. This tortured Kevin, sending him into a continuous spin, at a velocity which he had only seen world-class figure skaters achieve.

The music ended with a sudden, shuddering silence, halting its abuse of Kevin's body. He stood in the middle of his dance floor, sweating and gasping for air.

The crowd exploded into applause, whistling and hooting. For *him*. Even the mariachi band had set their instruments aside to clap for him. He turned his attention to Amy at their table, toward the street. She, too, was standing and clapping with a beaming smile. Another group of passersby had collected behind her, flocking along the cut-through street, cheering.

Kevin responded by being spontaneous, and doing what he felt was natural: he took a bow. He folded his hands together and shouted, "Thank you! Thank you!"

The audience's reaction was overwhelming. Kevin repeatedly saluted the people in gratitude. The applause finally receded.

"Please," he said, taking some paper bills from his wallet and raising it so that the entire crowd could see, "Please thank this incredible mariachi band!"

He handed the money to the mariachi leader. As others followed his example and overwhelmed the band, he took the opportunity to escape to the bathroom. En route, he noticed that the place had filled with patrons during his routine; perhaps the spectacle had given them the impression that Cantina Siesta was the place to be? In the bathroom he found an empty stall, closed the door, and jammed the earplugs into his ears, as far as they would go.

By the time he had returned to the patio, the crowd outside had dispersed and the band had resumed its pattern from table to table inside the restaurant. Resorting to the earplugs was an unfortunate setback, as he had been hoping to actually hear his conversation with Amy. His first lip-reading test-run with Amy at the funeral home a few days earlier had not gone very well. The disaster at the Martino funeral had further broken his confidence.

No longer one hundred percent sure of his ability to read lips, Kevin had prepared four phrases which he thought were "conversation proof": if he wasn't sure what the lips were saying, he could rely on any of these phrases to bail him out. He believed that they would suffice under any circumstance, during nearly any exchange:

1. "That's not important."
2. "I haven't thought about it that much."
3. "You tell me."
4. "What do you think?"

or,

5. Simply change subjects and say something about the food.

His fail-safe backup plan, in the event that if he did use one of these phrases and he could see from Amy's reaction that it was totally inappropriate or wasn't making sense, was:

6. Resort to laughing, as if he meant his comment as a joke.

For the most part, he planned to just let her talk. He would respond by nodding and every so often saying "Wow, really?"

The earplugs were well worth the money he'd spent on them: he could barely hear the mariachi band, which played to the indoor crowd for over an hour. After Kevin's show-stopping dance routine, the restaurant staff had left the door open, assuming that Amy and Kevin might want to hear their music on the patio. With his ears stuffed, however, the sound was so soft now that it only had minimal effect on his body. He thought this was perfect, since the gentle movement made him appear to be enjoying the music, yet did not overwhelm his ability to function. Amy even playfully mimicked his dancing a few times during the dinner.

As far as Kevin could tell, his strategy for the conversation was working:

When he didn't understand that she was asking him where he learned to dance, he answered, "That's not important."

When he couldn't figure out that she was talking about a new television series she had been watching, he said, "I haven't thought about it that much."

When she suggested that they order another round of drinks, he replied, "You tell me."

When she asked him if he liked his meal, he said, "What do you think?" Without hesitation, she took her fork, scooped a bite of his haddock, tasted it, and nodded.

When she was saying something about how much she appreciated his work for Esther's services, he commented on how tasty the potatoes were. She asked him if she could try some and he replied, "I haven't thought about it that much." She reacted with a confused look on her face, so he shrugged his shoulders and laughed. She returned the laugh and took a bite of his potatoes.

A few other exchanges didn't go so well, however:

When she was trying to let him know that it was getting chilly outside, he replied, "That's not important."

When he couldn't figure out that she was asking him how he first coped with his father's death, he said, "I haven't thought about it that much."

When she commented "Aren't these stars gorgeous tonight?" he replied "You tell me." She answered, "Well, yes, of course, that's why I was pointing that out," to which he nodded and said, "Wow, really?"

When she asked him if he was ever married, he responded, "What do you think?" This clearly confused her, so he asked her if her food was okay. She appeared to be saying something detailed about how it was cooked and perhaps the combination of spices, but he couldn't discern exactly what. She sat still, staring at him as if waiting for his reply. The only thing he could think of doing was shrugging his shoulders and laughing.

Despite his haste to finish the meal and leave the restaurant before the mariachi band had made its way through a second rotation, eventually the band did return for another round at their table on the patio. This time, however, Kevin's earplugs were snugly in place.

"Something soft, sweet, and slow," Kevin requested, before anybody could say anything.

The band broke into Roberto Cantoral's ballad "El Reloj." Before the song took hold of him, during the first few seconds, Kevin motioned with his hands, instructing them to play it even quieter. They obliged.

Still, Kevin's body rose from the table, albeit in a controllable state. He extended a hand to Amy, who accepted it and joined him on his dance floor. Kevin had no idea how to slow dance, so he let his body do whatever it may. Amy seemed to be thoroughly enjoying the unpredictable, yet easy, flow.

The wavelike movement of Kevin's arms captured the fluidity of the song, and managed Amy as if she were a wand in a wizard's hands. His heart jumped whenever he drew her body close to his. He devoured the scent of her perfume and savored her laugh as she rolled across his arms. Her eyes glowed with excited joy as he led her through a muddle of awkward dance steps. As they erratically sailed across the dance floor, Kevin realized something, and it frightened him: for the first time in his life, he didn't want a song to end.

But it did. Amy also expressed her disappointment that the song was so brief. He again thanked and tipped the band.

A few minutes later, they had paid the tab, left the restaurant, and were taking a stroll along the peacefully quiet beach. The only music was the crescendo of waves approaching the sand, collapsing with a thunderous clap, fizzling into salty foam, and then settling into a sweeping sheen as the ocean tugged its artwork back towards its core. Somewhere in there, Kevin stole a moment when Amy was distracted to remove the plugs from his ears. They talked about how much fun they had at Cantina Siesta. She told him that he danced like Luis Miguel. Having never heard of the famous Latin singer, he lied and told her that Miguel had a major influence over his style. They compared friends and relatives of around their same age; most had long since been married with kids. They talked about the stigma of being in their late-thirties and single. Once again, Amy told him that she admired his work at the funeral home. She told him about her position as a pharmacist and her former work as a nurse for a local hospital.

They laughed as they recalled Esther's descriptions about her relationship with Harry.

"You know," Amy said hesitantly, as if she was guarding her innermost thoughts, "I really like you. I'm glad we met. I don't want to come across too forward or anything, because we haven't known each other very long, but I hope you and I will have more than what they did."

"Well," Kevin joked, "It sounded to me like they were pretty happy with what they had going!" Then he paused, reached for her hand, and said, "But seriously. I hope so, too. I really like being with you. And in some ways, I think we already have more of a connection than they did."

It was nearly a perfect date, Kevin thought, as he drove home alone after walking her to her car. They hadn't kissed, but that was okay with him: they had danced and held hands in the moonlight. She had told him that she had a blast and hoped that they could go out again sometime. His head was delirious with joy.

However, there was something she said moments before he closed her car door that made him feel both ecstatic and uncomfortable: "You're so spontaneous. And unpredictable, in a fun way. I'm so glad I met you. I mean, other than the circumstances. It's strange how things happen sometimes."

TWELVE

Kevin spent two full days in the Neurology Department at Massachusetts General Hospital, once again submitting himself to test after test, screen after screen, expert after expert. And that was after spending a full day in the Psychiatry Neuroimaging Laboratory at Brigham and Women's Hospital across town. Brigham and Women's had referred him to the MGH specialist after determining that its results were inconclusive other than narrowing the number of causes down to a few possibilities. The MGH Neurology team also reviewed all of his medical history, particularly that from recent months.

Dr. Dansoff, Director of MGH Neurology and one of the premiere neurologists in the world, began the appointment by mentioning that he recognized Kevin from YouTube. "Someone posted a video of you as the Mariachi Dancing Machine. Now I understand where you get your dancing style.

"Yours is without question one of the most unusual cases we've ever seen," Dr. Dansoff said as he delved into his prognosis. "As a matter of fact, to many neurologists, your condition exists only in myth: there have only been eighteen documented cases…since 1787. That is, the year 1787."

"Lucky me," Kevin said.

"Well, I guess, if your goal in life is to be on every talk show, you will certainly accomplish that," Dansoff replied. Kevin couldn't tell if he was joking or not.

"Now, Kevin," the doctor continued, "There are some strange, but well-known dancing…disorders…and symptoms…if you will; historically, this is nothing new.

The Shakers, for example, held group sessions in which they believed shaking…often induced by dancing…was a spiritual phenomenon, sort of like an enlightening. And in the seventeenth century, there was a disease called Sydenham's chorea: its symptoms were jerky movements in the face and limbs that some people referred to as dancing.

"Today, many of the experts in this field suspect that some of those historical cases were either dramatic, consciously-controlled episodes, or, that perhaps early diagnoses involving chorea may actually have been epileptic seizures. One of our colleagues suggested you might have some complicated form of Huntington's disease, but your blood tests ruled that out immediately.

"I could get into the details of everything we've considered and tested, but to cut to the chase, I can tell you that within eighty-five percent certainty, we have determined that you are suffering from something that, at the moment, only two other people in the entire world have: Musica Chorea.

"Wow. Imagine that."

"Yes, imagine."

"What did you say it's called, 'Musica Chorea'?"

"Yes, dancing movement brought on by musical sounds. Of the eighteen documented cases, each one has the same thing in common: the symptoms began after a severe physically traumatic event. In each event there was something that likely caused some spinal and/or brain injury. For example: a fall from a three-story building, a climbing accident, or exposure to a massive explosion. In your case, the car crash. So every single person who has had this disease had a terrible accident, a result of which we believe there is some neurological impairment related to the brain's interpretation of auditory signals. We think that somehow the basal ganglia has been affected."

"The what?"

"Basal ganglia. I guess you could say, in the simplest sense, that it's a part of your brain that helps to control your movement. It makes sense of signals and then tells your body what to do with them. We just haven't had enough cases to fully test the disease, and frankly, it's so rare that it's unfortunately not worth the resources of most research facilities. Besides, it's very difficult if not impossible to detect, even with sophisticated imaging we have today.

"Incredibly fascinating disease though. I am honored to meet you."

"Thanks?"

"Oh, no problem, the pleasure is all mine. Now, here is the situation Kevin: because we still don't know exactly how this disease works, we don't know how to treat it. There have been some pretty radical approaches. In 1842, one patient in France agreed to have his auditory canals permanently sealed, in an attempt to block the noise. It worked, but he died five weeks later. Several patients have tried to remain dangerously heavily sedated when they know they will be around music. For example, while on a train or traveling through a thickly-inhabited area, they would have someone wheel them along while they remained, basically, in a temporary coma. This merely minimizes the intensity of the movement, while making the patient oblivious to what his or her body is doing. In another case, a man relocated to a remote location in Siberia, where he was sure that there was virtually no sound at all."

"Why am I dancing? I mean, as opposed to shaking, or falling into a trance?"

"Nobody knows for sure. How can I explain this, simply? Well, it's like this: people suspect that the brain sends a signal through the nerves that triggers a sort of muscular impulse, more or less. It's possible that this impulse is triggered somewhere in your subconscious, where your brain has also stored memories of dance movements that you've experienced in the past, in one form or another, whether you've performed those moves yourself or seen someone else or watched a video."

"Is it potentially fatal?"

"Well… it's not likely, but yes, if the circumstances are right, yes."

"And what are the 'right' circumstances?"

"Well, if you are in poor physical condition and in a situation where loud music is played constantly. If you're trapped in an elevator and it is blasting fast-paced disco music, there might not be any way out for you."

"But being trapped in an elevator that is blasting disco music would kill just about *anyone*," Kevin contested.

"True. But you get the idea."

"And there is no cure?"

"There is one known cure, we think, but are not sure."

"That's encouraging."

"There was one case about eighty years ago when a patient couldn't take it anymore. He was scheduled for a lobotomy, but then realized that that might be worse than the relentless dancing. So he tried to take his own life and jumped off a sixty-foot cliff."

There was an uncomfortable pause as the doctor allowed Kevin to digest the story.

"So, you're saying I need to try and kill myself in order to get rid of it?"

"No. Again, we only have one record of a cure, so it is difficult to draw any conclusions. This patient survived the jump, but suffered serious injuries, and those did turn out to be fatal about two weeks later. But for those two weeks, he appeared to be completely free of the disease. The conclusion, some of us believe, is that the only cure for Musica Chorea is to suffer an equally physically-traumatic event. We don't recommend this, of course, but we do know that at least in the case of this one patient, the severe trauma from his jump cured it."

Kevin sat in the chair, dejected. Only eighteen rare cases. No treatment. The only cure is uncertain, painful, and potentially fatal.

"What *do* you recommend, then?" he asked after accepting the heartbreaking conclusion.

"Wear earplugs, learn to read lips, learn sign language, avoid music, and learn how to dance. So you don't end up hurting yourself when you're having a seizure."

Kevin sat in dismayed disbelief.

"It's not all bad," the doctor continued.

"How's that?"

"Believe it or not, this actually qualifies you for a handicapped license plate, so you'll have ideal parking options from now on."

"Awesome," he apathetically commented.

As he left the center, he replayed the doctor's words in his head, *"The only cure for Musica Chorea is to suffer an equally physically-traumatic event."* If this disease continued to take a toll on his life, he wondered, could he, or would he, ever make an attempt like the patient who jumped from the cliff?

THIRTEEN

While Kevin was finally getting answers from Dr. Dansoff about his mystery ailment, McCormick Funeral Home had held the wake for Yolanda Bliss, a gospel instructor from Boyd's church. Yolanda was a close friend of the Oakleys, particularly Boyd's wife, Anita, who sang in their church choir on occasion. She was seventy-three years old. She had suffered a stroke, fallen into a coma, and remained on life support for a week before her children unanimously decided to have her removed from it. She had left that decision with her eldest son, Jamal, but he insisted that all six of her children—four boys and two girls—arrive at a decision together. Having watched her suffering increase as her condition deteriorated, it took them less than five minutes to agree.

Yolanda's husband Clinton died of pneumonia four years prior. He worked in the Converse shoe factory plant decades ago before becoming a minister at the First Baptist Congregation on Main Street in Malden. The Blisses had always been very active in the community, promoting various causes and making sure their voices were heard at local political events.

After leaving Dr. Dansoff's office, Kevin arrived at Yolanda's wake as it was nearing its end. It was strangely silent. Boyd and Anita were still at the funeral home to support the family, but also because Boyd wanted to help personally oversee the services of his wife's friend. Kevin took Boyd aside for a moment to reveal his diagnosis.

"'Musica Chorea.' It's extremely rare, only three or four known cases in the entire world today," Kevin said, explaining his dancing disorder.

Boyd stood, apparently dumbfounded, intently listening as Kevin explained the disease, how it worked, what causes the seizures, and so forth. Boyd rubbed his chin, absorbing the news. Boyd was a sharp dresser, especially at these types of events, at which he typically wore an impeccably wrinkle-free suit, perfectly creased pants, and gold cufflinks with the musical treble clef symbol. Aside from his wedding ring, in recent years Boyd began to wear a gold ring on his right hand as well. The ring was also gold, with a section of a musical staff, the treble clef, and a couple of notes, one of which was marked with the sharp symbol. Sprinkled into this design were some small diamonds. The ring was a gift from Kevin's father to Boyd, commemorating his twenty-fifth anniversary with McCormick Funeral Home in 1999.

"The only known cure is to suffer an equally physically traumatic event," Kevin said. "So, for now, all I can do is wear earplugs and avoid music."

Boyd continued his confused stare, trying to digest the information. As he pressed a finger to his lip and rubbed his chin, his anniversary ring sparkled, catching some of the candlelight from Yolanda's remembrance.

"Boyd?"

Boyd remained speechless, shaking his head in disbelief.

"Boyd? What are you thinking?"

"Well," Boyd answered, collecting himself, "I think you should embrace it."

"Embrace it? Are you crazy?"

"No. I think you should embrace it. I think it's no coincidence that you were in your father's car when this all happened. It's almost like your father was taking the car away and leaving you with something better, something that would be…more fulfilling."

"Fulfilling? Boyd, I can't walk down the street or do my job or anything without worrying about whether or not I'm going to have a dancing attack or not. My life is completely destroyed!"

"Well, I'm sorry Kevin, but I think just the opposite. I think you've been given a gift. What a beautiful way to experience life."

"Boyd, you have no idea what I've been going through."

"If you can't accept it, then you shouldn't be at the funeral tomorrow. Why don't you sit this one out: there will be more music there than you can handle."

Kevin agreed. The funeral was expected to be laden with gospel music, given Yolanda's musical influence over the years. Dooley and Barry should be able to handle things, and Boyd would be present in case anything went awry. Dooley, Barry, and Boyd assured him that they would have everything under control. Kevin was somewhat skeptical, especially because Boyd never took part in the funeral itself; he was primarily responsible for embalming, cosmetology, and cremation.

*   *   *

The first thing that went awry for Yolanda's funeral was that Dooley and Barry had forgotten her sunflower bouquets. Sunflowers were her favorite, and her six children had pitched in to buy her an extravagant arrangement that was expected to remain beside her casket during the funeral and would also be present for the graveside prayers.

At home, sitting in perfect, peaceful silence, Kevin got the call from Dooley:

"We're heading to the church in the hearse, leading the funeral procession from the home, but we just realized that we forgot to bring the sunflower bouquet. So it's not like we can turn the whole procession around to go back and get those flowers. Can you run and pick it up, set it on the altar?"

On the one hand Kevin was exasperated that they had overlooked that critical detail, but on the other hand he wasn't surprised. Dooley told Kevin that he would drive extra slowly, ensuring that there would be enough time to execute the errand.

"By the time we get there," Dooley assured him, "You'll be long gone."

Kevin dressed in a black suit and brought his earplugs along, in case something else that required his urgent attention occurred. Sure enough, something did: by the time he had retrieved the flowers and delivered them to the church, he noticed that some people had already arrived, apparently bypassing the automobile procession. He heard some people complain that the hearse was driving so slowly, they weren't sure if it would ever make it to the church. The first four rows of pews, which had been designated for the Bliss family still in the procession, were filled with mourners. After Kevin set the bouquet on the altar, he went to address the guests that were seated in this family area.

He learned that some of the guests were actually family, but others not, and sorted out the confusion. However, no sooner had he directed the non-family mourners to other seats than another group of people had also arrived and tried to seat themselves in the family area, ignoring the ribbons that marked those pews.

A lot of people sure felt close to this woman.

He decided to wait around to explain the seating arrangement until the procession arrived. While he was directing traffic, the preacher tapped him on the shoulder and asked him if he had a program that included readings and hymns scheduled for the funeral.

"We seem to have misplaced the program," the preacher explained, "We don't know who's doing what."

The preacher also requested that Kevin identity those people who were involved in leading certain parts of the funeral and to seat them specifically, where he could call on them.

"There are so many people that are going to be here, so many people that will want to say something," he said.

Kevin realized he wasn't going anywhere. For one thing, he couldn't identify anyone until they arrived. He shoved the earplugs into his head and prepared to ride out the impending hurricane.

This is Boyd's friend; I can't let this get screwed up.

As the procession arrived and more mourners began to pour into the church, Kevin took his place toward the front pews to direct traffic and to identify certain people. Toward the back of the church, Dooley and Barry appeared shocked when they noticed Kevin. Boyd covered his mouth in startled disapproval. Kevin simply acknowledged them by nodding and waving a hand, letting them know that he had everything under control.

The funeral began beautifully, the four sons acting as pallbearers, assisted by Dooley and Barry, the casket wheeled towards the altar along to the slow, soothing hymn "It Is Well with My Soul." Kevin had located a program from one of the family members and passed it along to the preacher, who smoothly guided the congregation through two scripture readings, a somber, steady rendition of "Down by the Riverside," sung by a member of the choir, another reading, and then an explosive sermon by the preacher himself.

Kevin never had much trouble with allergies to flowers, but for some reason his nose would not stop itching, and as the service progressed it became increasingly irritated. He discreetly scratched it and moved to the other side of the altar, where he believed he would be safely far from whatever seemed to be aggravating his nasal passages.

Although the earplugs muffled the preacher's voice, and there were parts of the sermon that Kevin could not hear at all, most of it was loud and articulated enough that

Kevin could understand it. The preacher hailed Yolanda's spirit, her impact on the community, how she gave people a voice through her teaching of gospel music. He described how he imagined Clinton and Yolanda "seated at the table of Jesus at this very moment," and how "their love is showering us all, at this very moment." He described her grace, her love of people, her patience with anyone who wanted to participate in the choir, and how "that patience fueled the passion and love that fills this church every Sunday." He was an excellent speaker and clearly trying to inspire the crowd.

The itchy sensation in Kevin's nose refused to subside. He never had much trouble with flowers in the past. He borrowed a tissue from one of the mourners and tried to subtly rid his nose of whatever allergy was stimulating the mucous, which was now building in his nostrils.

What struck Kevin about the ceremony, however, was how flatly the mourners responded. The atmosphere was dark and dreary. He imagined how drained the family must have been after Yolanda's week-long coma; most of these people probably had little to no sleep as they contemplated the impending death of their unconscious mother, unable to offer her any words of consolation, seeing her breathe yet knowing they would never speak to her again. He thought of the strength it took for the choir to deliver the songs that Yolanda had taught them.

After the preacher finished his sermon, he called on two of the choir members, the oldest and youngest, to take the podium. The oldest member was a heavy-set, fifty-year-old man with a deep, full voice. The youngest was a nine-year-old girl who had joined the choir less than a year prior. The two members read a thank-you note that the choir had collectively prepared: it was a list of memories and lessons that Yolanda had taught the group, balanced with both humorous anecdotes and very serious stories. Each of the two members took turns reading "thank you for…."

"…not being upset with me when I forgot the words to 'I'm Free' even after you went over them with me twenty times…"

"…telling Billy not to eat any more before our performances…"

"…acting as if you didn't notice how many notes I missed during the Christmas vigil…"

"…sharing your heart with us…"

"…inviting us into your world of music…"

After each memory, the congregation mumbled a lackluster "Amen."

The itching in Kevin's runny nose would not relent. Still, he believed he had it under control and that the issue was only temporary.

The two choir members finished the note and reassumed their places among the rest of the group. Promptly, the choir broke into a lively version of the Hank Williams gospel song "I Saw the Light."

The itching suddenly drove along the bridge in Kevin's nose, travelling to its crest between his eyes. He closed his eyes and held his breath to try and block the sneeze, but that only increased its force. The expulsion echoed throughout the church, leaving his head in a fog, and for a split second he thought that the choir paused mid-chorus.

The itching was gone, thankfully. Kevin drew a deep breath and exhaled it; he was relieved—until, after the next eight seconds, he realized that he could hear the music a little too well.

What? Did I lose one of…?

He put a hand to his right ear, the one which seemed to be capturing most, if not all, of the sound. The earplug was gone.

The sneeze must have knocked it loose!

As he swiveled his head to try and locate the missing earplug, his other hand desperately dove into the breast pocket of his suit to find the spare set of earplugs.

It was too late. His shoulders shrugged along to the beat, his spine rocking his body back and forth. His feet began to scamper across the front of the church along to the rhythm of the piano. The spare packet of earplugs, which he barely managed to retrieve from his suit pocket, flung out of his hand and went sailing into the crowd, never to be seen again.

Noticing Kevin's behavior, the confused choir at first began to unravel. A few of them stopped singing altogether. The piano player, whose back was to the crowd, had no idea what was happening and continued to pound away at the keys. The drummer only seemed encouraged that at least one person in the audience was enjoying the beat, and started to play louder. The preacher, who had been trying to awaken the crowd since the service began, walked towards Kevin, bending his knees while clapping to the beat.

As he reeled across the front aisle, Kevin saw a few faces begin to boil, angry at his sudden, inappropriate display of disrespect towards Yolanda's remembrance. His memory flashed to images of Don taking measures in the confessional booth.

Sitting in the first pew, Jamal stood, shouted, "Amen!" and joined the preacher's clapping. Influenced by this alternative perspective, the angry faces began to soften.

Motivated by the sudden life in the church, the choir regrouped, blending sounds harmoniously, as they accelerated the pace of the song and belted it out with soulful enthusiasm. Kevin's body spun around the front of the church, then launched itself down the main aisle, mixing random leaps with a bumpy, jive dance. The preacher's booming vocals joined the choir in singing the chorus.

The first few pews hesitantly rose to their feet, clapping, dancing, and singing. The rest of the rows followed, like a wave at a sporting event. With the entire church on its feet, the choir extended the song, repeating the chorus.

At some point during the shuffling, spinning, and hip-quaking, Kevin's eyes caught a glimpse of Boyd, who was seated in a pew directly behind the family's designated area. Boyd was standing, perfectly still. Like much of the congregation, his eyes were transfixed on Kevin. Unlike much of the congregation, which was singing and rocking to the music, Boyd simply grinned, contently watching Kevin.

When the song finally ended, Kevin collapsed onto an unsuspecting middle-aged man in one of the pews. He had the attention of the entire church. Several of the choir members came toward him, one burying his shoulder into one of Kevin's armpits to support his body, as they all led him to their platform near the altar.

"No," Kevin panted, "I can't go up there, really…I have a heart condition…I have to leave…."

"Don't be silly," one of them laughed, "Do you know 'I'll Fly Away'?"

"No, no, no. I think it's time for me to head out now."

"That's okay," another choir member told him, "You can just dance along to it, like you just did."

Jamal delivered the main eulogy, which was followed by more words of commemoration from Yolanda's two daughters. As the three of them closed their speech, they thanked "Brother Kevin for reminding us all of what Yolanda was all about: the power and spirit of song." A few people even clapped. Kevin noticed Boyd actually clapping and laughing simultaneously. Kevin sat restlessly with the choir, scanning the ground for his lost earplugs.

Yolanda's children stepped down from the podium, each gently kissing her casket. Dooley and Barry directed her four sons to their positions around the casket. The audience stood. The piano began a solo introduction before the calamity of Albert Brumley's "I'll Fly Away" began.

Kevin's body launched itself into motion as the crowd joined the choir in singing the chorus.

The pallbearers led the casket down the center aisle. Kevin danced uncontrollably near the altar. Someone shoved him forward, directing him behind the casket as it rolled out of the church. The choir and preacher followed Kevin, initiating a dancing procession. One by one, the pews emptied into the parade of clapping, singing, and dancing. Each time Kevin's momentum carried him astray, one of the choir members would steer him back into place, behind Yolanda.

The parade collected outside the church, surrounding the casket before it was loaded into the hearse on its way to the cemetery. The mass of mourners finished singing the song. Once again Kevin fought to catch his breath and temper his heart rate.

As he propped himself up against a railing for support, an older, burly man embraced him and said, "Thank you! This was the best funeral of all time!"

An elderly woman approached him and wept, "What a wonderful, wonderful thing you did here today."

"Great service! Great job!" one of the family members shouted.

A choir member firmly shook his hand and said, "She would have been so, so proud."

One of the percussionists asked him where he learned to dance.

Watching this barrage of praise was Boyd, waiting patiently for his turn to comment, while standing about ten feet from Kevin. As the mourners dispersed to join the automobile procession to the grave, Boyd repeated the words of the burly old man, "'The best funeral of all time.' Did you hear what he said?"

As his panting subsided, Kevin looked up at his elder, long-time friend, "Yeah."

Boyd stated authoritatively, "A gift."

FOURTEEN

Except for his struggles with Musica Chorea, things were improving for Kevin. Incredibly, he had survived a few more dates with Amy. They made a return trip to Newburyport Beach for a quiet afternoon picnic on the sand. They went for a peaceful stroll through Boston Common and across Boston Public Garden, taking a ride on one of the Swan Boats and finishing with hot chocolate from a park vendor's booth. She had been to his house, which of course was completely disinfected from any musical germs. She even stopped by the funeral home a couple of times to join him for workday lunches.

He knew that this romantic fortune would inevitably expire. Amy was, after all, in an elite class of desirable singles. Moreover, she was enamored with music. Each time they met, she would make some reference to music she liked and performers she wanted to see. She begged him to go dancing again. He promised her that he would, time permitting. That unfulfilled promise, he believed, was the carrot that was keeping her interested in him. At some point, he would have to reveal his music problem to her. It was becoming increasingly challenging to make up excuses and avoid being around music with her. He was convinced that once his secret was disclosed, and she realized the truth about how much he disliked music, she would leave him.

For now, he was content to enjoy the veiled romance as much as he was capitalizing on the sudden infusion of new clients for the McCormick Funeral Home. After Yolanda's funeral, business exploded. Word spread about Kevin's lively, celebratory funeral style. Overnight it seemed, he had become somewhat of an internet sensation, at least in the world of death and funeral bloggers. Inquiries for death and funeral arrangements didn't double: they quadrupled. Some of the requests were borderline offensive:

"I really want my grandmother to go out with a bang," was how one woman began her call.

"It's got to be like a Grateful Dead show," described a middle-aged man, who was preparing services for his comatose, diabetic father.

"I want everyone to get crazy and party down," said another man, dying of cancer.

Kevin had several one-on-one discussions with members of his staff to gauge how they felt about these new, odd inquiries. Nearly everyone encouraged him to accommodate as many as he could, so long as the services weren't vulgar or completely inappropriate. They liked the idea of exploring this direction for the business, despite the challenges it would create for Kevin. Everyone seemed to express a concern for the decline in business in recent years and how it made them fear for their jobs. They did not associate the slowdown to Harry's death; rather, they attributed it to a shift in social trends.

"Seems like more and more people these days prefer a simple remembrance and go straight to the crematorium," Boyd remarked. "I never understood why funerals have to be so sad and morbid myself. I mean, you should either be rejoicing because someone's gone to heaven, or you want people to celebrate your life. Either way, the dark depression that people sink into for these events doesn't make sense. I can see why more and more people are moving away from it.

"Listen to what these people are asking," Boyd advised him, "You're delivering more than just a product off an assembly line."

Kevin listened and worked diligently to determine the best course to try and manage the new flood of unique business. Although he was still not entirely sure if the venture would succeed in the long run, he hired some temporary help: two assistant funeral planners, a cosmetician, and another administrative assistant to help Missy. Some of the work, such as cremations, headstone designs, and casket ordering, was outsourced or simply referred to other firms with some revenue-sharing agreement. It seemed liked Kevin was hiring someone new every other day. Even Dotty had to hire a couple of new florists to handle the overlap into her flower boutique.

The most peculiar new hires, however, were for something he never imagined would be central to a funeral service: dancers. Many of the new requests for services asked specifically for some kind of musical arrangement, featuring the favorite music of the deceased, performed live if possible and with some sort of choreographed routine. Finding bands and musicians wasn't a problem at all given Boyd's and Dooley's contacts. Some people even explicitly requested Yolanda's choir group, after seeing them perform on YouTube. The dancing, however, was something with which nobody had much experience.

Boyd suggested that Kevin contact the Berklee College of Music in Boston and see if any professors could recommend dance groups or choreographers that might be interested in performing part-time at funerals. The Director of Dance, Tai Randall, was not only intrigued with the idea, but she also mentioned that the faculty for years had been considering offering a class about dance as an art form celebrating death. She noted that in some cultures, especially ancient Latin America, Africa, and even for some Native Americans, certain dance rituals were associated with death.

"The problem is," Randall explained, "that although dance was important in an historical context, much of the faculty disagree that it is worthy of an entire semester, given the absence of dance at funerals in our country today. It simply doesn't have a practical implication. For a week or two, it is interesting to discuss, but for an entire semester, dance students are better off studying and training in different areas."

Kevin tried to narrow her perspective, saying, "Look, I'm not looking for students to perform Aztec rituals. All we need is a few dance students who are looking for some low-paying part-time work—interns or something."

Randall insisted that Kevin make a trip to Berklee to discuss the idea more openly with the college's Department of Dance faculty. Boyd laughed boisterously when he learned that Kevin was going to visit the campus.

"You? You're actually going to visit that place? That's like a Red Sox fan going to Yankee Stadium. You better take Dooley, because there will be music everywhere. Ev…ery…where."

Boyd was right: on a warm September afternoon, as Kevin and Dooley walked from a Boylston Street parking garage to the hall where he was scheduled to meet the professors, Berklee musicians littered the sidewalk. He passed a group of college women practicing their vocals, a solo saxophone player trying to collect donations from passersby, and a jazz quartet jamming out a tune outside of a CVS pharmacy. One of the busiest areas he passed was outside of the Guitar Center instrument supply store, where one group of students was practicing singing and dancing, while another was comparing electric guitars. The store itself had a steady flow of traffic. His heart raced with anxiety, as everywhere he turned, someone was either singing, dancing, or toying with a musical instrument.

Good thing I'm wearing my earplugs.

"See, man," Dooley remarked as they passed a pencil-thin man, covered head-to-toe including his clothing in silver paint, dancing alone on the sidewalk for spare change, "you fit right in here!"

"Dooley," Kevin replied, "This place is my worst nightmare."

The location of the meeting was The Loft, a Berklee dance hall that was also designed to host live performances. Walking through the building toward The Loft, Kevin shuddered as they passed a room full of students learning to play keyboards: thankfully the glass wall was soundproof. They passed another room full of electronic recording equipment: Kevin was grateful that everyone working inside was wearing headphones. The Loft itself resembled a gymnasium with a high ceiling and hardwood floor. Each step echoed as they walked across the room. The Berklee officials were seated at folding tables towards one end of room.

A wiry-lean woman, who had the appearance of someone who spends far too much time in aerobics classes, came toward them. She was wearing a tight shirt that hugged her flat stomach. Her snug jeans accentuated the toned muscles of her legs. "Dr. Randall," she introduced herself as she extended a hand.

'Doctor'? You can be a Doctor of Music?

"Dooley Hammond," Dooley said as Kevin contemplated the doctor title. "I am so, so, so honored to meet you!"

"Kevin McCormick, Director of McCormick Funeral Home," Kevin finally uttered, shaking hands with each Berklee representative.

One of them, introducing himself as "Dean Coltrane," asked for Boyd, saying that he knew Boyd "from the music scene back in the day."

Why am I not surprised?

Randall explained that the group represented a panel that the school had assembled to consider Kevin's proposal. Kevin and Dooley took their seats across from the panel. Except for the sounds of voices rebounding from the walls of the room, it was wonderfully silent. Kevin removed his earplugs and stuffed them into one of his pockets. As they listened to the school's concept of a collaborative course with the funeral home, Kevin reiterated, pleadingly, that all he needed was a few students who wanted to make some extra income for dancing at funerals.

"But we saw your video," Randall said, "And we believe that you are onto something bigger."

"Our video?" Kevin corrected her, "Understand, we didn't put any videos out there. Whatever you've seen is something that we haven't approved."

Dean Coltrane interjected, saying that some of the most valuable lessons learned in college are *life* lessons, and that a course held in conjunction with McCormick Funeral Home would "open students' eyes to life experiences unlike any other course we have to offer. Commemorating death through dance is, celebrating the essence of life." He stated that he was not surprised that there has a growing market for Kevin's particular brand of funerals.

"Using dance to offer students a certain closeness with the recently deceased is a powerful idea," Coltrane said.

"What a beautiful way to remember, and honor, our lost loved ones: through song and dance," Randall elaborated.

Then Randall asked a question that Kevin never would have expected in his wildest dreams:

"Where did you learn how to dance?"

Dooley also apparently did not expect that question; looking towards Kevin, his eyes popped open and his lower jaw caved in, as if he had eaten a sourball.

"I'm…I'm…self-taught," Kevin finally answered.

Dooley quivered, trying to hold off his laughter.

"Interesting. The reason I ask is because there is so much originality in your work."

Again, Kevin turned towards Dooley, who was wincing to keep a straight face.

"Thank you, thank you," Kevin said. "It's nice to be acknowledged for that."

"Would you like to see something he's been working on?" Dooley suddenly offered.

"What?" Kevin retorted.

"We'd love to!" Randall replied. The rest of the faculty agreed.

"No. Not now. What? No. I'm not ready yet," Kevin rambled, unsure of where Dooley was going with this.

"Oh...you're ready," Dooley insisted, "We had an agreement, remember? The agreement?"

Kevin gazed at him, puzzled. *Agreement?*

"About the phone call to Amy?" Dooley reminded him. "We came to a certain understanding, about a time and place."

"Oh, right," Kevin said, recalling the bet he'd made with Dooley weeks ago: if Dooley was correct, then Kevin would have to dance at a random time and place, and to a song, of Dooley's choosing. "But I'm not sure this is the time or place, though," he rebuked.

"Oh, believe me, I think this is the perfect place," Dooley argued with a mischievous grin. "In fact, I don't think I could have imagined a more perfect setting."

A bet is a bet, and I am a man of my word.

"Okay," Kevin said quietly with a knot in his throat, "Let me show you...what I have been...working on."

"Awesome, awesome!" Dooley cheered, standing from his chair and retrieving his phone.

He moved some chairs out of Kevin's way and instructed him to stand in the center of the room. The panel sat curiously patient, each one of them leaning eagerly forward, as Kevin stood still, arms by his sides, with a rueful glare towards Dooley. Before he started the music from his phone, Dooley took one chair and slid it towards the middle of the room, next to Kevin. Then he

142

scrolled through his phone's music library, propped the device on one of the desks, and set a song into motion.

Kevin recognized it after the opening strolling, strutting drum-like sound, leading into the first few notes. In a panic, he changed his mind about honoring the bet. He started walking toward the phone to turn it off before it was too late. This time Dooley had gone too far; it was Michael Sembello's "Maniac," a song written for the 1980s film "Flashdance," about an aspiring female dancer. Kevin had seen the movie in his youth, remembering it primarily because of what he regarded as the foolishness of the Maniac scene. More than music itself, he hated the music montages made famous by the eighties films. He also believed "Flashdance" was one of the key experiences that fostered his disdain for popular music. He had shared his view of the song and movie with Dooley many times over the years, particularly in their youth.

By the time Kevin had taken six steps towards the phone, which was by then about an arm's length away, his body had surrendered to the beat. Dooley had turned the volume as loud as it could go. Kevin's arms, legs, back, neck, and head broke into full, erratic motion, held only in place by the structure of the song.

He was gone to the music, knees high-stepping, arms flailing, head veering backwards.

Well played, Dooley, he thought as he slid across the floor on his knees to the second verse. *Perhaps the most humiliating experience of my life!*

As his body relentlessly strutted and twirled out of control, Kevin couldn't help but be fascinated at how much his moves reminded him of the movie, which he hadn't thought about in over a decade, at least. It was as if his body was delivering some kind of mystical memory recall. He ran in place, high-stepping to the beat, pumped his fists in the air, and at one point even outstretched his arms, finger-pointing sequentially to each person in the room. An attempted backflip didn't work out quiet as well as his body had planned. Incredibly, however, his body just kept going, without missing a single beat. As he succumbed to the quick, repeated, contorting movements—his mind in another dimension than his body—he also recalled the only redeeming quality of the movie: its beautiful star Jennifer Beals. He remembered her character's dance moves on the chair and at once realized with horror why Dooley had placed it on the dance floor.

There was nothing he could do. His body spun towards the chair, resting his shoulders at the top of the backrest, arching his back upward, his memory replaying whatever it could recall. He knew that the water-splashing image was associated with the movie's other famous song, "Flashdance—What a Feeling" by Irene Cara, but his body didn't seem to understand the difference—or care—and promptly reenacted the body thrust regardless.

At least I'm not getting pelted by a bucket of water.

The entire panel wildly applauded.

Kevin finished the song with another knee-slide across the floor, ending near the tables at which the panel was now standing. They erupted into cheers and clapping as he rose to his feet, wheezing and sweating.

"Remarkable! Remarkable!" Randall said.

"Look," Dean Coltrane implored, "If the point you're trying to make is that you'd like to help out on the choreography, by all means, of course we'd be open to that." The rest of the staff nodded in agreement.

"Water! Water!" Kevin gasped.

Somewhere amidst his fight for breath and hydration, Dooley's sly grinning, and the Berklee's staff's showering praise of his performance, Kevin agreed that McCormick Funeral Home would participate in a dance co-operative program with the Berklee College of Music. In the days that followed Berklee's press release about the new program, at least one news outlet featured it among its evening stories, describing it as "a controversial yet groundbreaking approach to mourning."

Thanks, Boyd.

FIFTEEN

Even for someone who thoroughly enjoys music and dancing, the stresses of Musica Chorea at times can be mentally and emotionally crippling. As if being around dancers, musicians, musical references, and an embalmer who requires music at work wasn't enough for Kevin, much of his free time was being spent trying to pretend to Amy that he loved music.

The funerals had turned into small productions, and the few that they'd conducted through the co-op program drew crowds as large as any that he'd ever seen at a McCormick Funeral Home service. One funeral was even reviewed on the "Performing Arts" webpage of Boston.com. The steady attention created a burgeoning wave of business, causing Kevin to offer two of the temporary employees full-time positions while hiring three more staff members. Dooley had to commit one hundred percent of his time supporting Boyd as an assistant embalmer/cosmetician.

One Friday night that October, Kevin desperately needed relief from his exposure to music. He was dreading his planned date with Amy, which was sure to include more excuses and lies to hide his condition. They had tickets to a stand-up comedy show at the Orpheum in Boston: another event with minimal use of song. The venue also offered food: a convenient excuse to avoid dining at a restaurant.

The show was great, with five comedians performing at twenty-minute intervals. Between acts, the house played no more than fifteen seconds of music. During the acts there was nothing but talking: no props or skits involving music. Kevin was armed with a few sets of earplugs as a precaution.

At the end of the show, Amy insisted on going dancing, or at least stopping by a bar that had live music. Kevin adamantly refused, saying—lying—that he had a throbbing headache and that he was exhausted from a long week at work.

"We'll go tomorrow night," he suggested, unsure of how he was going to accomplish that.

"All right, but I don't want any excuses tomorrow about headaches or how tired you are or how much you've been around music, okay?"

"Okay."

As he drove home to the lonely sound of a hybrid automobile, curiosity led him to pose the question that he had previously only asked while preparing for someone's funeral:

"Amy?"

"Yes?"

"What's your favorite kind of music?"

"I never told you?" she said, surprised.

"No. I know your mom liked jazz and swing, from what she told me in the hospital, but you never told me what kind of stuff *you* really like."

"I like everything, really: jazz, swing, rock, dance, blues, rhythm-and-blues, even some rap," she answered, "But I would have to say my go-to music, the songs I listen to more than anything, is reggae."

"Really? Reggae? I should have guessed that."

"Why, do you know much reggae?"

"No, not really. I know what it sounds like, in general, and have heard it in Jamaica and Hawaii, but I never really got into it."

"I love tropical places."

"Me too. I love the quiet scenery along the beaches, especially. They're the perfect places to clear your head, get away from your anxieties."

"For sure, I agree. But it's too bad you haven't warmed up to reggae. You don't know what you're missing: Jimmy Cliff, Bob Marley, Yellowman, Toots and The Maytals, Peter Tosh. Here, let me show you..." She reached for the button on the radio.

"No, that's okay," Kevin said as she pressed a button on the panel and began to adjust the tuner.

"Just a second, I always listen to this channel, let me get it…"

"Amy, really, please don't."

"What's wrong with you?" she snickered, "I just want you to hear some of it for one second. It might be good for you, help you let go of your stress."

Ignoring him, Amy continued to adjust the tuner on the radio until she found her station. A light, steady song came on the radio. Kevin recognized the words, but he had never heard a reggae version. It was "Ain't Too Proud To Beg," by The Temptations, a Motown hit from the sixties about a man who refused to accept that his romantic relationship had ended. The radio was playing a "cover": a copy or "remake" of the song recorded by another artist.

"Oh, wow, this is a classic," Amy said excitedly, "Do you know Slim Smith? This is Slim Smith."

Although the music was mellow, with a relaxing effect as Amy predicted, Kevin's body caught the rhythm and started to bob in the front seat. It was the trigger that caused Kevin to snap after weeks of wrestling with Musica Chorea and deceiving Amy. He turned the music off before his body was completely overtaken and swerved the car to the side of the road, abruptly parking it. He disengaged the ignition key.

"Slim…Smith? You have a problem with that song?" Amy asked, baffled.

"No, I never heard of him."

"That's classic reggae," she started, but evidently she sensed that something else wasn't right. "What is wrong with you tonight?"

It was the first time he had seen her even mildly perturbed.

"Look, it's not just tonight. It's *every* night. Every single day since I met you," he said.

"What?" she exclaimed, shaking her head in confusion.

He noticed her breathing becoming heavier in her emotional anticipation. "Listen, Amy," he said in a sharp, condescending tone, "I don't like music. At all. I can't listen to it. It actually, truly, makes me…sick. Sick."

It came out rudely and disrespectfully. The frustration from the disease had finally burst his restraint. But it was out: he couldn't retrieve it now.

"Where is this coming from?! I mean, but you dance? You dance…all the time. You danced all through my mother's wake. And funeral. And you were just now dancing to 'Ain't Too Proud To Beg.' I don't get it." Her disposition shifted from confused to angry, "Is this some kind of excuse to call this off?"

"It's not an excuse, Amy. I don't dance. I don't. I've hated music ever since high school."

"I don't believe you. *Who* hates music?" Tears formed in her eyes as she calmed herself and asked, bracing for a painful explanation, "What's the problem, really?"

"That's it. What you've seen, up until that first day we met, is not me. I have a disease, ever since the car accident. It makes me dance whenever I hear music."

Her forehead creased and her teeth clenched as she glared at him. Her attempt at sensibility was yielding again to anger.

"It's true. I've been pretending to like music the whole time."

"If you're trying to end this," she chastised him, "you don't have to do it with such a crazy story, Kevin."

He reached into his pocket and removed a wad or earplugs.

"Look: why else would I need these?" He opened the glove compartment, which held a pile of new earplug packages. "You don't know me, Amy. The guy you've been spending all this time with has a complete, passionate loathing for music. There is no cure for this disease."

She rolled her eyes and scowled.

"Do you believe me?"

"No."

"If you turn that music back on, I will not be able control myself. I will start dancing, and there won't be anything I can do about it until the music stops."

"If it's true, then why didn't you tell me weeks ago, or at some point over the past couple of months?"

"Because I knew that's why you liked me: because you thought I loved music and dancing. The truth is I hate both, Amy. But I am so far out of your league, I just couldn't bring myself to say 'no' to you. You're so great when you're having fun, smiling, laughing. You're amazing; I knew I was unworthy the whole time. I was counting my blessings to be able to be with you, but the whole time I knew it was going to end at some point, when you realized I have Musica Chorea."

"Music what?"

"*Music-a* Chorea. That's the disease. Musica Chorea."

"You know I've been in the medical field for fifteen years."

"Yes," he acknowledged.

"And you're still trying to convince me of this…idiotic nonsense?"

He sighed. "No, I'm not."

"Is it because I like reggae?"

"No. Look: everything I told you is true. Everything. Being around you makes me want to like music. But you don't know me. This whole…relationship…was just about me being selfish."

"Just take me home."

*   *   *

The ride to Amy's house was tensely silent. Amy stared out her window on the passenger side. The route took them along the Fellsway: the scene of Kevin's fateful crash. As he glanced towards the cluster of trees that left him with the dancing disease, he recalled Dr. Dansoff's theory that suffering an equally traumatic experience might cure it.

I survived it once; I could survive it again.

Kevin drove slowly, hoping Amy would say something, but even when he parked the car in front of her condo complex, she didn't utter a word. She simply opened the car door, got out, and closed it behind her.

That evening, strangely, he preferred to go to the funeral home than his own house. He sat in his office, for hours, wide awake, reliving the moments he shared with Amy. He wished he had told her from the beginning, but after seeing how much she loved music, he knew things would have ended much sooner. He rested his feet on his desk, staring at the ceiling, at his blank computer monitor, out the window, and at the pictures on his walls. He dozed off briefly here and there, but for the most part he sat and stared off into space, taking stock of the past few weeks, wondering if he was ever going to get another shot with someone like her.

Is she really worth it?

It was music, once again. Music was his only enemy; it inevitably seemed to find diabolical ways to mess with his life. He thought again about the trees along the

Fellsway: the route to the disease could be the route to its cure.

SIXTEEN

Kevin had sat in his office for the entire night, contemplating everything. As the orange-red hue of dawn peeked through the night sky outside his window, he heard the lock to the front door disengage along with the jingling of keys. The home's main door creaked open, followed by Boyd's merry whistling. He heard Boyd's happy, energetic footsteps thump down the stairs, toward the offices, heading to his embalming room. Kevin needed someone to help him snap out of his depressed trance. He decided to hurry after Boyd before he started his music.

Not realizing anyone else was inside the building, Boyd had left the door open as he began his work. As he was about to turn on his stereo, his back turned towards the entrance, and he caught a glimpse of Kevin. He spun around and screamed in fright.

"My god, Kevin," he exclaimed, "I thought you were a corpse that must have gotten up or something! What are you doing here? It's not even seven o'clock! I didn't see your car out there."

"Sorry about that. My car's in the back. What are you doing here?"

"I had some things to finish up before the funeral later this morning," Boyd answered, motioning to the body on the table.

Kevin thought that the man looked lifelike. *Impressive job, once again.* "He looks good to me," he responded.

"No, not quite," Boyd disagreed, "I was up all night, tossing and turning about this one. Wasn't happy with how he looked."

"Who is he?"

"His name is Derek James. He was seventy-eight-years-old. Died of a brain tumor. Real estate developer. Owned a property management company for about thirty years. He liked Cream, Traffic, Led Zeppelin, The Yardbirds. Big Jeff Beck fan."

"Who?"

"Jeff Beck."

Kevin shook his head, indicating that he was unaware of a "Jeff Beck."

"Are you serious, Kevin?"

"Yes. Sorry, never heard of him."

Boyd held his breath for a moment and shuddered. He took a deep breath, pointed to a chair and ordered, "Sit down."

Kevin followed his instructions.

"Jeff Beck," Boyd began, "is one of the most accomplished, versatile guitarists…ever. His career as an instrumentalist is…a hallmark in perseverance. His music has laced virtually the entire span of rock and roll. He has been playing with various headliners since the 1960s. He played with Eric Clapton and Jimmy Page, all three from the Yardbirds, all three of whom are in the Rock 'n Roll Hall of Fame."

"The *what* birds?"

"Yardbirds. Are you kidding me?"

"No."

Boyd released a slow, exasperated breath.

"I'm listening," Kevin coaxed him to continue, "I'm genuinely listening."

"The Yardbirds. One of the foundations of classic electric rock guitar. Jeff Beck. From there he started his own group with Rod Stewart and Ron Wood of the Rolling Stones: also both in the Hall of Fame. He's played with Keith Moon, drummer for Led Zeppelin, Hall of Fame, Roger Waters of Pink Floyd, Kate Bush, Paul Rodgers of Bad Company, Sting, Mick Jagger, Phil

Collins of Genesis, Bob Geldof. He's also played with the likes of Kelly Clarkson, Joss Stone, Stevie Wonder, Jon Bon Jovi, Herbie Hancock, Joe Cocker, Cyndi Lauper, Buddy Guy, Seal, Tina Turner. Any of these ring a bell?"

"Yeah, sure."

"Shall I go on?"

"No, I get it."

Boyd weighed Kevin's response, assessing its sincerity before remarking, "No you don't. The man has several gold, platinum albums, several Grammy awards to his credit. He's cracked the Billboard charts several times in each decade since he began recording in the late 1960's."

"Okay, okay, I'm impressed," Kevin interrupted, unimpressed, but trying to humor Boyd enough that he could change the subject.

"Even if you tried," Boyd lectured, "You cannot fully appreciate the legacy of his music, his sound. This is a man who's ridden the rock 'n roll highway since before you were born, and along the way he's paved some of it himself. All the peaks and valleys, the latest trends, the most highly respected musicians: he's been there throughout. One of the most influential guitarists—musicians—of his era."

"Yeah," Kevin interrupted again, "I get it: he came up with something that could sell records and then a whole bunch of other people copied it. I know how it works."

"No," Boyd stopped him, raising a palm as if to silence him. "You don't even know what you're talking about. It's all connected, in a way that you don't appreciate. It's not about 'copying' so much. One musician influences and inspires the next…perpetuating a constant weaving of styles and techniques that are all connected. Each introduces his or her own uniqueness, but together it's…well…an evolving, spiritual exchange.

"The Yardbirds, for example, were named for the jazz musician Charlie 'Yardbird' Parker. Do you understand? They were influenced by the early sixties blues artists like Muddy Waters, Chuck Berry, and Bo Diddley. These were the people that took a blues sound and transformed it into the roots of rock. It inspired Jimi Hendrix, Elvis Presley, B.B. King, and even The Beatles, all of whom influenced countless musicians. Lots of people liked it and made it their own. Berry covered a couple of Waters tunes himself.

"I'm assuming you know who Chuck Berry is?"

"Yeah, I think I've heard of him."

"You think you've 'heard of him'? You're musically ignorant, Kevin. You really are. You need to learn something if you're going to run this business the way it's going."

"Okay," Kevin exhaled, relinquishing his ears to Boyd's teaching, "Tell me about him."

"Yes, yes, I will," Boyd said, one step ahead of him. "Chuck Berry changed the world," he began, then paused, letting the statement resonate. "He changed…the…world."

Kevin couldn't help but laugh. "Come on, Boyd, it's not like he invented the wheel or cured polio or won World War II. So the guy was a star for a while in the fifties. Big deal."

Boyd clenched his teeth in frustration. "Let me tell you a story about a man named Chuck Berry from St. Louis, Missouri."

"Boyd, really, I've got to get to work."

"No," Boyd insisted, "You will sit there and listen.

"Chuck Berry did 'Brown-Eyed Handsome Man,' which was covered by many bands from Elvis Presley to Buddy Holly to Lyle Lovett to Paul McCartney. You know, Paul McCartney, of The Beatles?"

"Sure."

"Well, you could put an entire album together with all of the Chuck Berry songs that The Beatles covered. 'Carol,' 'I'm Talking About You,' 'I Got to Find My Baby,' 'Little Queenie,' to name a few. 'Little Queenie' has been one of Berry's most frequently covered songs, with remakes by REO Speedwagon, Jerry Lee Lewis, and The Rolling Stones. You *have* heard of the Rolling Stones, haven't you?"

"Of course."

"Okay, well, between The Rolling Stones and its members' covers of Berry, you have at least six or seven remakes. Led Zeppelin: equivalent to another entire Berry remake album. Even The Doors did a cover of 'Carol.'

"I need to show you something," he said as he walked towards his computer, which contained his endless library of songs organized according to whatever categories suited him.

"I have a category here," Boyd said, sifting through computer folders, "entitled 'Old School Rock 'n Roll Remakes'," he noted. "Let me read to you some of the songs:

"'You Never Can Tell,' by Aaron Neville. Guess who did that song originally?"

"I don't know."

"Chuck Berry. Here's another: 'Too Much Monkey Business' by The Yardbirds. Any clue on who did that one first?"

"Not a clue."

"Chuck Berry. Also covered by the Kinks. Let's try again: 'School Days' by AC/DC."

"Never heard it."

"Chuck Berry. How about 'Nadine' by Bob Dylan?"

"No idea."

"Chuck Berry. Okay, let's try 'Memphis' by Roy Orbison, 'Johnny B. Goode' by Phish, and the same song by Elton John?"

Kevin shrugged his shoulders, although he was starting to get the hint.

"Chuck Berry, Chuck Berry, Chuck Berry. Peter Tosh covered 'Johnny B. Goode' too. Let's see…'Round and Round' by David Bowie, 'Route 66' by The Replacements, and also by Nat King Cole, 'Rip It Up' by Little Richard, 'Around and Around' by The Grateful Dead, and the same song by the Animals. Wanna guess?"

"I probably can."

"You guessed it: all Chuck Berry covers."

"Is that all?" Kevin asked, rising from the chair, teasing Boyd as if he was bored and unaffected. Kevin wanted to say that he wasn't surprised—that Boyd was only proving his long-held belief that most popular music was simply the manipulative mechanism of commercially-driven minds—but he sat, listening quietly, hoping that Boyd's speech would end.

Boyd took a deep breath and turned to his computer screen one last time, "'Back in the U.S.A' by Bruce Springsteen, also by Linda Ronstadt, and also Southside Johnny, 'Johnny B. Goode' by Judas Priest, 'Come On' by Joe Jackson, also by The Sex Pistols, also by Living Colour, and while we're at it: Jimi Hendrix. And The Beach Boys, who also covered 'Rock and Roll Music.' 'Let it Rock' by Bob Seger, 'Sweet Little Rock 'n Roller' by Rod Stewart, 'Sweet Little Sixteen' by The Animals, 'No Particular Place to Go' by The Troggs, who also covered 'Memphis,' 'Roll Over Beethoven' by ELO, 'Promised Land' by James Taylor, 'Maybelline' by Foghat, 'Let It Rock' by The Georgia Satellites, and Dave Edmunds…my God that guy could have his own box set of Chuck Berry cover songs! Let's see, what else…'Havana Moon' by Levon Helms…"

"Boyd!" Kevin interrupted. Now, even to a music hater, it was an amazing list. Even Kevin had heard of many of these artists.

"I'm not done yet. I haven't even gotten into all of the covers that Danny Fallon's done. I've got at least fifty, sixty more here."

Wow. "Sixty more?"

"At least."

Kevin sat back into the chair. "That really is unbelievable. I had no idea. Maybe he did change the world. And so, who did you say it was, one of the bird guys, that took this blues-rock sound and made it contemporary?"

"The Yardbirds," Boyd continued, "Well they were at least one of the groups that developed its sound. Jeff Beck, Eric Clapton, and Jimmy Page. Extraordinary to think of the impact that they would have on the world. And the life experiences that would inspire their music. That is it, Kevin—not only is it talent and determination that made these people successful, but also their soul-shedding that you hear in their music.

"They actually developed a rivalry—Clapton and Beck—that lasted for decades. Sort of evolved from a clash of styles. But the soul-shedding made the music. Clapton alone poured a wealth of emotion into his music. Never knew his father. Thought his mother was his sister until he was nine, because he was raised by his grandparents. The guy saw many of his fellow musicians die well before their times, in various circumstances: Duane Allman, Jimi Hendrix, John Lennon, Stevie Ray Vaughan. He fell in love with one of his best friends' wives. He fought a heroin addiction. 'Layla.' 'Wonderful Tonight.' Masterpieces. Charged with emotional depth.

"Then, Kevin, here we have this man—Clapton—who finally decides to bury his demons and fulfill his role as a father to his four-year-old son. The day after he conveys this to the mother of his child, the boy falls to his death from a New York skyscraper window."

Boyd paused, letting Kevin absorb the weight of the tragedy.

"Can you imagine," he implored of Kevin, "the emotion that was poured into that song 'Tears in Heaven'? You've heard it, I assume?"

"Yes, I've heard it," Kevin recalled Clapton's monster hit from the nineties. He never knew what the song was about, having dismissed it years ago as just another pop jingle. Boyd's explanation, however, numbed his skull and ran through his veins like ice water.

"And you don't get it?"

"I've heard it," he muttered, "but I never really listened to it very closely."

"The man is a legend," Boyd stated. "Seventeen Grammy Awards. He's overcome tragedy, drugs, alcohol, depression, again and again. Some of the best-selling albums and songs worldwide. He's recorded and performed live with more people that you can recall: The Beatles, Elton John, Phil Collins, Tina Turner, Dire Straits, Blind Faith, Neil Young, Tom Petty, Chuck Leavell, Toots and The Maytals, Bob Dylan, The Band, Duane Allman, John Lennon, Sting, Aretha Franklin, Dr. John, George Harrison, Frank Zappa, Bob Geldof, Lionel Richie, Santana, Paul McCartney, Mary J. Blige, Carol King, Waylon Jennings, Junior Wells…."

"Boyd, Boyd," Kevin interrupted, shaking his head in disbelief.

"How many people can say they dated Janis Joplin *and* Sheryl Crow?"

Wow, really? Kevin sat in awe, his mouth open.

"One. Yes, really." Boyd laughed. "I doubt Mr. Clapton can even recall himself all of the people he's played with. Now, imagine the trials and tribulations, the emotional ups and downs that Clapton emptied into his music over the years. And people pick up on it, cover it, or incorporate it into their own music. It's like, 'Hey, I like your song, and this is how I interpret it.'"

Kevin didn't know all of the stories behind Clapton's music, but the weight of message was starting to reach him.

"It's a sharing of life experience. The best music results from liberation of emotion. You can't have that without real-life experiences. And the best live performances are ones when musicians leave a piece of themselves on stage."

Kevin nodded his head, trying to understand.

"Now," Boyd said as he put latex gloves onto his hands, "Derek James here understood that, appreciated it, and devoured their music. So that is why I couldn't sleep last night. Because I understand how that music reached this man, and I didn't feel that I captured enough of who he was."

"Okay," Kevin concluded, standing, "I'm going to go home and take a shower."

"A shower?" Boyd echoed in a confused tone. His eyes rolled over Kevin's crumpled outfit, and he asked with piercing concern, "Isn't that what you were wearing when you left here last night?"

"Yep," Kevin frowned.

It was then when Boyd first acknowledged Kevin's rough appearance. "How long have you been here? You *do* look like hell."

"Since about midnight."

"But I thought you had a date last night?"

"I did."

"She ended it?"

"*I* ended it."

"What?!" he shouted. "Are you crazy?"

"Yes, I am. And that explains it."

"You told her, about the dancing?"

"Yep."

"You know, I don't understand why you didn't tell her in the first place."

"Yeah, I know," Kevin said in desolate reflection. "And you know what? It was stupid. Because if I had just told her the truth up front…you know she has this amazing quality: she seems to be able to overlook people's biggest flaws. In a weird way, I think that's what she really *likes* about people: their flaws."

"*That's* obvious," Boyd snickered, "She's dating *you* after all."

"Boyd, please, I'm hurting here."

"I can see that. So tell me what happened. You told her about the disease, and she didn't like it?"

"No. She didn't believe me."

"Why not?"

"Because I told her it's not who I am. Told her I don't like music, don't like dancing. She didn't believe me."

Boyd stepped closer and looked sternly into Kevin's eyes. "Kevin: it *is* who you are. Like it or not, it *is* who you are. This is part of you now. They told you there is no cure. A lot of people, in case you haven't noticed, really like this 'problem' of yours. Including me. Now, you've found someone you're crazy about, and she happens to love something that you think is your greatest flaw. Do you know how lucky you are? You think you're a monster, but she loves all the 'scary' features you're worried about. And she's crazy about it. She begs you to go dancing every time you see her.

"I told you once, and I am going to tell you it one last time, if there is nothing you ever hear from me in your foolish head, at least hear this: you have a gift, something you should embrace. You connect with people in a powerful, spiritual way through this gift. There is a whole, wonderful world waiting for you out there. You're robbing yourself of…*life*."

Kevin was starting to wonder if Boyd was right.

"I would be taking dancing lessons if I were you," Boyd remarked as he turned towards his computer, preparing to set a playlist in motion. "Go home and take your shower; you need it!"

SEVENTEEN

Kevin sat in an old 1973 Ford Pinto, parked on a side of the Lynn Fells Parkway, less than a mile from the very scene of his fateful crash that first led to his dancing disease. The Pinto model was a compact, two-door sedan that gained notoriety for its poor safety design, its rear window sloping down directly from behind the front seats, into the bumper. It was a design all but guaranteed to suffer severe damage during any crash. Kevin thought about how much his life had changed since his car veered off into the woods weeks ago. He thought about how that one event had turned his life upside down:

He had destroyed his father's prized Cadillac.

He'd been humiliated repeatedly by the uncontrollable dancing episodes.

He'd been accused of having a crush on his mother.

His business was now spiraling into a direction that contradicted his long-held convictions regarding music.

He'd not only suffered physical abuse from the seizures, but he'd also been assaulted by mafia men and even a priest.

He would never overcome the psychological damage of performing "Maniac" in front of a panel of academics at Berklee.

What felt worst of all, however, was that he'd blown a chance at a relationship with Amy, the likes of whom he would certainly never meet again.

He recalled the words of Dr. Dansoff from Neurology at Mass General, when he explained that one patient "tried to kill himself and jumped off a sixty-foot cliff." He survived the fall, at least for a few days, but the trauma did appear to cure the disease: the only known case in which a patient was cured from it. Members of the medical community who examined and re-examined that man's case were not entirely sure that it was actually the trauma itself that fixed the problem, it was only a hypothesis.

Still, Kevin was willing to try it. He had been quietly considering that option now for the last two weeks. The events of the past few days had heightened the urgency to put the trauma theory to the test. He sat in the motionless car, studying the curve ahead, where the road disappeared into a blind stretch. It was the exact curve that led to this mess. The process would be simple, he imagined: he would travel at the same speed as before, make a similar sharp turn at the same point along the road, thus launching the car into the same block of trees. The only difference would be that now he was in this tiny Pinto, which was about half the size of the late 1980s-era Cadillac. For that reason, maybe he'd reduce the speed. He had bought the old car, which was made before air bags became standard on automobiles, specifically for this purpose.

There were three most probable outcomes for this event:

1. Death.
2. Cure.
3. No cure, but a result which wouldn't leave him in much worse condition than he was already experiencing. In fact, he believed that if he still had the disease but was left paralyzed from the crash, it would be an improvement.

Oddly enough, death would result in the least amount of trouble. If the crash cured the disease, assuming he didn't end up with any permanent injuries, his life would resume its previous course with a struggling business and a lonely, boring, single lifestyle. If it didn't cure the disease, he'd still be the same prancing, spinning, gyrating novelty act, with the bane of his existence now driving his business, and again with the same lonely, boring, single lifestyle. He accepted the fact that in either case he would probably end up with some new injuries.

Kevin stepped on the gas, revving the engine. It didn't quite have the same effect as the old car. It actually felt pathetically powerless.

He pressed his hands against the windshield; he wanted to assess whether it would shatter on impact.

He knocked on his head; he wondered if it would withstand a collision with the windshield.

He patted the zippered breast pocket of his jacket; he wanted to make sure that his wallet was safely tucked away, but in an accessible place, so that he could be easily identified.

He unlocked the doors; this way emergency crews would have less difficulty in getting his body out of the destroyed car.

He checked the gas gage; it was nearly empty, so if there was an explosion or leak it wouldn't be very big. In their time, Pintos had a reputation for gas explosions.

He thought about the gas again; he wondered if there was even any truth to that gas explosion on impact stuff that he had often seen on television.

He checked to make sure that the seatbelt was fastened; that would help to ensure his survival.

He unbuckled the seatbelt; for a moment he decided that he might not want to survive.

He buckled the belt again; he wondered how well these old seatbelts worked in the first place.

He looked into the mirror and adjusted his hair; he wasn't sure why he did that.

Kevin steadied himself, gripped the steering wheel, and tested the gas pedal once again. He hoped that the car wouldn't stall halfway through the turn. Still, after all of his preparations, something didn't feel right. He thought about his mother, Dooley, Boyd, and the others at the home whose lives relied on his business. He thought about Amy, and what she might think after she heard that he had intentionally driven an old Pinto into a wall of trees.

No, I've got to try something else first, before I go down this road.

Kevin withdrew his phone from one of his coat pockets and dialed Dooley.

"Kev, where are you? We've been trying to get a hold of you all day! The phone is ringing off the hook, and we've got clients all over the place!"

"I'm on the Lynn Fells Parkway."

"On your way here?"

"No. I'm parked on the side of the road."

"What?"

"I'm just sitting here, staring down the road."

"Why? Is there an accident? Flat tire? Did the car die or something?"

"No. Nothing like that. Dooley, I need you to get over here right away. Forget about the business for now. I have something else I need to take care of, right now."

"What is it?"

Kevin paused before answering, unsure of exactly what it was he needed to do.

"Kev?" Dooley asked, breaking the silence.

"Dooley, I'm about to do something…completely irrational. You might even say it's insane. But it's something I need to do."

"Okay?" Dooley said in a tone that invited Kevin to elaborate.

"Dooley, I'm going to try something," he grappled for the right words to convey the gravity of his situation, but could only produce the single phrase that weighed most heavily on his conscience: "and I'm not sure I'm going to survive it."

EIGHTEEN

Sitting in the Pinto on the Parkway, Kevin watched as Dooley drove past him a few times before Kevin realized that his friend would be looking for the new hybrid Toyota, rather than an old Ford. Dooley had never seen this car. Kevin had purchased the Pinto for this one-time shot at driving it off the road. Kevin phoned him to let him know that he was looking for the wrong vehicle.

"Damn, Kev, where did you get this thing?" Dooley asked after he eventually circled back to Kevin and parked his car behind the Pinto.

"Ebay."

"What happened to the Prius?"

"Nothing. I didn't need it for this."

"For what?"

"I wanted to drive this off the road."

"Yeah, I can see what you mean. You've probably bought one of the only vintage automobiles that has no resale value whatsoever."

"I know. I actually got it for a dollar."

"You were robbed. So what's up? Did it break down?"

"No. I really mean it: I really did buy it to drive it off the side of the road."

Dooley studied Kevin for a moment, digesting that response. "You okay?"

"No!" Kevin cried, distraught. "I don't know how to function anymore. Everything's gotten so out of control, making me do things I'd never imagined."

Dooley reacted with a heightened urgency, apparently realizing that Kevin was actually going to try to demolish the car and perhaps himself in the process.

He rested a hand on Kevin's shoulder and calmly told him to take a deep breath.

"This is not rational, Kev. Let me have the keys."

"Rational? You want to talk about rational? How rational is it that your body bursts out dancing every time you hear a note or a drumbeat?"

"Yeah, but that's no reason to kill yourself, buddy."

"I wasn't going to kill myself."

Dooley seemed confused. "Then what were you doing?"

"The only potential cure to this thing is physical trauma. So I was going to try and crash this thing the same way, the same type of crash that caused the disease in the first place. I thought that might knock it out of me once and for all."

"Or kill you."

"Yeah, possibly. That felt like a nice option about an hour ago, when I was considering it. But that's not why I called you here."

Dooley was clearly struggling to understand. "But you said on the phone that you were going to try something, and that you might not survive. And so I show up here, and you're telling me that you've been thinking about driving an old Pinto into some tree trunks. But now it's something else? You're losing me, Kev," he said, exasperated.

"Yeah, I know, I know. That was the plan before I called you. But then as I was thinking about everything, I thought about what Boyd said: 'Embrace it.' And you know what? I have to admit, I did have fun at the Yolanda Bliss funeral. And I laugh whenever I think that Berklee of all places would want *me* to be part of a *dancing* co-op. And I did like some of Martino's opera music."

He slumped forward in dejection, before continuing, "But the best...was with Amy. You should have seen the look on her face when I danced to that Latin cockroach song at Cantina Fiesta. It was awesome dancing with her, the way she reacted, how happy she was, just us being spontaneous and fun."

"I know," Dooley confirmed, "Everyone thinks you're a total jackass for dumping her."

"Well, I am. I'm an idiot. I had something great going, and I didn't get it. So I'm sitting there in this musty-smelling, rusty, old, brown Pinto, thinking, 'What else can I do?' before trying this last resort of driving a deathtrap through some trees. And that's when I came up with this idea. It's desperate, and dangerous, at least because of my condition. So I wanted you to be there in case it starts to go all wrong."

*   *   *

The two friends took Dooley's car, leaving the Pinto on the side of the road. It was Amy's day off. Kevin knew that she had previously planned to spend the day at her condominium with a friend. Kevin and Dooley drove to her complex and spotted her car in the lot.

"You ever hear of a reggae singer named 'Slim'…something or other?" Kevin asked Dooley.

"Slim Smith?"

"Yep, that's him."

"Of course. One of the original reggae acts. Dozens of recordings…famous stuff… maybe even a hundred songs. Died when he was in his twenties though. Came home from a party, realized he'd locked himself out, then decides to break into his own home by punching his way through a glass window. He ended up bleeding to death. Why? You're not thinking about breaking into her condo or anything, are you?"

"No, of course not. I wouldn't do anything illegal like that."

"But *stalking* her is okay?" Dooley mocked him.

"Well, yes, I guess I forgot to tell you that we might get arrested for this."

"Thanks, Kev."

"Sorry. Anyway, Amy likes this guy Slim Smith, and he has this song I've heard before, at least I've heard the words. I know you have one of those high-end stereo systems set up in here. So I want you to blast this song on your stereo, while I go out onto the courtyard over there, in front of all the condos, and sing and dance to it."

Dooley laughed. "Are you out of your mind?"

"Yes," Kevin replied with a stone-serious face.

"Which song?"

Kevin sang the first few words. "I don't know all the words, but I want to try and fake it."

"'Ain't To Proud To Beg'? Outstanding. But there are other versions out there, too. You know the Temptations originally did it. That might be a better fit for you." Dooley began searching through song titles on his smartphone. He played snippets from a Temptations version as well as another by The Rolling Stones.

"Let's do the Temptations one," Kevin decided. At least he had some familiarity with that one.

Kevin walked to the middle of the courtyard, facing the back of a string of about eight connected condominiums. To his left were six more condos, behind him eight more, and to his right even more. In the complex there were also two other similarly arranged blocks of condos, about sixty altogether.

"Amy!" he shouted.

No answer.

"Amy!"

No answer.

"AMY!!!"

There was no sign of any reaction from the windows of Amy's house. A few of her neighbors, however, heard him shouting and were peeking through their windows.

"Okay Amy! I know you're in there!" he shouted. "I saw your car in the lot. I just wanted to say that I'm an idiot. A complete jackass. I have no idea what I was thinking about."

"Hey, watch your mouth!" a woman walking by with a young child scolded him.

"Sorry," he apologized. "Amy, I just wanted to let you know that I am going to try and work through this thing. And I'm going to start with something for you. Okay, Dooley, start it up!"

Dooley had lowered all of the windows in his car, so that the music would carry through the entire neighborhood. The plan was to let Kevin sing the first few lines on his own.

The music kicked in from Dooley's stereo. Kevin's body picked up the rhythm, alternating between strutting and shifting his hips from side to side, the swing of his arms testing his balance. He didn't know all of the words, but faked them as much as he could. He did recall the chorus and made sure that he belted it as loud as his voice-box could handle.

About halfway through the song, a police cruiser eased into the parking lot, flashing its lights as it parked next to Dooley's car. Between Kevin's uncontrollable motion and unpredictable step patterns, he could see that Dooley noticed the police car approaching. Dooley walked away from his own car, pretending to the officer that he did not know whose car it was. Dooley pointed towards Kevin, perhaps suggesting to the cop that it was Kevin's vehicle. Dooley tried to distract the man for as long as he could, but eventually the officer started walking towards Kevin.

As the song ended, the cop approached Kevin and said, "Let's go buddy, party's over."

"What? I'm just dancing," Kevin pleaded.

"Well, some of these residents are complaining that you're being vulgar and creating a disturbance, that's what," the officer explained.

"No, he's with me!" a woman's hoarse voice interrupted from one of the balconies.

Kevin looked to the source. It was a large—very large—middle-aged woman with rough, wiry hair, missing teeth, and wearing an oversized sweatsuit.

"What?" Kevin asked.

"Who are you?" the officer questioned her.

"I'm Amy," the thing replied, "He was singing to me."

"No, no, I wasn't," Kevin whispered to the policeman.

"It's okay, I believe you," the officer murmured in response.

"He's with me, actually," another voice chimed in from an adjacent lot.

It was Amy Best. She was walking through the visitors' parking lot with her friend.

"It's okay, officer," the real Amy smiled, calming the confusion with her soothing presence, "*I'm* Amy. He's with me."

"Okay," the officer said. It was difficult to argue with Amy's charm. "Look, buddy," he ordered Kevin, "Turn your car off and get out of this courtyard. If I get another call I'll have to come take you in."

"No problem, sir. I'm sorry for the trouble."

But he really wasn't sorry at all. The "disturbance" had brought him back to Amy, who appeared anxious to talk.

"How much did you see?" he asked her.

"Some of it. Most of it." She laughed. "It was great."

"Thanks. Did you hear what I said? At the beginning?"

"No. But I looked into the disease, your Musica Chorea. I can't believe it. It all makes sense now. But I'm

173

glad you came back. I'm sorry I didn't believe you. I always thought you were one in a million, but after reading about that disease I guess you could say you're one in…billions?"

"Thanks."

"What did you say? At the beginning?"

"I said that I'm not going to fight this thing anymore. But I think I'm going to need you to help me through it."

"Well, you have me."

"I don't want to lose you," he said, seizing her by the arm and yanking her towards him, "If it means I have to dance to keep you, then…" he dipped her backwards, holding her spine parallel to the ground as he leaned over her, and looked into her eyes, "I *must* dance!"

She laughed as he maintained a playful, yet sincere stare.

"Kevin?" she asked, as if she was wondering if he was ever going to raise her body upright.

"I'm not going to let myself lose you again," he said intently.

"Okay. I don't want to lose you either."

He swung her body upright.

"Wait a minute—there's one more thing," he noted, suddenly leading her body into another dip. This time, however, he held her more tightly, pressing his upper body against hers and firmly wrapping his arms around her. He finished the sequence with his finest dance move yet: a gentle kiss that barely met her lips. It seemed to catch her off guard first, but she quickly, readily, returned his invitation, melding her mouth against his, encouraging the initial contact towards a more passionate mingling of lips, tongues, and saliva.

NINETEEN

Boyd Oakley died on an unusually mild Wednesday morning in October, a week before his seventy-fourth birthday. He was getting dressed for work in his bedroom on the second floor of his home, when he called out to Anita, who was making coffee downstairs. Anita would later explain to Kevin and others at the funeral home that she replied "What is it Boyd? What?" thinking that he'd lost his belt again or something, before she strolled to the bottom of the stairs.

When she approached the stairs, she saw Boyd, clenching his teeth, wincing in pain, with one hand clutching his white dress shirt. With his other hand, he reached for the bannister and tried to take a step. Suddenly, Anita said, his eyes closed, his head sunk to his chest, and he fell. It wasn't a terribly violent fall: he sort of plopped into the bannister, slid against it awkwardly, tried to continue down the stairs, stumbled, and flipped over towards the bottom step, landing almost at Anita's feet.

"It all happened so quickly, I never expected him to fall," Anita sobbed as she described the scene to Kevin.

Anita raced for the phone to call 9-1-1, then returned to the staircase, where Boyd lay motionless. She sat on the floor beside him shouting his name, trying to wake him. She managed to lift his upper body enough to rest his head on her lap.

"I begged him, 'Boyd, Boyd, please wake up!'"

Boyd finally lifted his eyelids a small crack, enough so that she could see him looking at her. His raised his left arm, the one that was closest to her, and gently touched the side of her face. He didn't say anything. They stared at each other for the last time, Boyd peeking through his half-shut eyelids.

"It was a look," she wept, "That only two souls, who shared the world together, could understand."

After a few seconds, his eyes closed for good, his arm falling limp.

It was most likely a heart attack, the hospital later reported. She didn't want an autopsy.

"It was no matter. He was gone. Cutting him up to figure out why it happened wasn't going to do me any good."

Contemplating the news, Kevin sat in his office, stunned. He had just worked alongside Boyd only yesterday. There were no signs of anything wrong. Boyd had left at around four o'clock in the afternoon, his usual self, whistling, stopping by Kevin's office briefly to poke his head in and say, "I'll be seeing you, dancing fool."

Kevin had no idea those would be the last words he would hear from him.

Now Kevin had a job to do, but what awaited him was beyond vocation. This would be very personal. He would be sending off a part of himself.

"You know he loved you, like his own son," Anita stated. "He always said that if there was someone he could trust to see him off the right way, it was you, Dooley, and the people in this home here."

"I know," Kevin replied, "We will take good care of him. Give him what he deserves."

"I think you'd have a good idea of what he might like. You knew him as well as anybody."

"He mentioned some things here and there."

They *had* actually talked about it, to an extent, several times over the years. It was inevitable conversation around the funeral home to discuss what one's own arrangements would be like. Usually they would joke about it, but within the banter there were some serious revelations. Because of his age, Boyd had actually gone so far as to complete the entire McCormick Funeral Home arrangements packet: selecting flowers, the coffin, the style of headstone, his burial plot, some background to mention in the obituary, and some particulars regarding the service itself.

Kevin had never read it until now. When he opened Boyd's folder, he noticed three words, all in bold-faced, enlarged, capital letters, etched beneath his name, address, contacts, and so forth:

"NEW ORLEANS FUNERAL"

Kevin smiled and nodded. He had heard of the unique practice in New Orleans that involved a parade of somber music, typically played by drums and horns, following the casket through the streets.

Perfect.

"What is it?" Anita asked.

"Have you ever seen this packet?"

"No, never. Didn't want to think about it. He always told me I wouldn't have to worry about a thing except the obituary and how to spend all of his insurance money."

That sounded like a Boyd quote. Kevin handed her the paper and pointed to the header that Boyd had written.

She grinned, "Oh yes, we talked about this, years ago. He said it might throw you for a loop, but it would be wonderful."

She wiped her tears, reflecting on the conversation she had with her husband, "You know, he wanted a certain style of music. He may have written something about that. He didn't want it to be so slow and sad."

Kevin referred to the packet again. Sure enough, one of the next pieces of paper was a hand-written note by Boyd, with a list of songs, each of which he had added "in the style of" and the name of a musician. Kevin flipped through the papers. Boyd was thorough and creative. He had made it easy for them, even suggesting names of some local musicians, including their phone numbers and instruments.

There was one certain detail, however, that surprised and overwhelmed Kevin with urgent purpose. It was written at the end of Boyd's funeral outline, following titles of specific psalms to be read and hymns to be sung. There, at the very bottom of the funeral mass section, Boyd had handwritten, so that there would be no mistake:

"Eulogy to be delivered by Kevin McCormick."

*   *   *

Immediately after Boyd's passing, Kevin handed the embalming reins to Dooley. Boyd was one of the first clients under Dooley's direction. Dooley tried his best with Boyd's body, but he couldn't handle the preparation alone and had to enlist the help of an outside embalmer. Dooley was certainly skillfully qualified, talented, and had enough experience to take those reins, but this one proved to be too emotionally challenging.

When Kevin inspected the presentation of Boyd's body in the casket prior to the viewing service, he felt—oddly—overjoyed with how peaceful and content Boyd appeared. Kevin swore that it looked as if Boyd was trying to hide that playful, warm grin that had enriched the funeral home for all those years. There was a sense that Boyd was resting, relaxed, eyes closed as if he was trying to absorb the melody of another song. His old trumpet was standing upright outside of the casket.

Dooley had slightly modified the casket with the help of one of his engraving artist friends. The two of them designed a thin brass band that wrapped around the outside of the casket. Imprinted in this band were the notes to the melody of Sam Cooke's "A Change Is Gonna Come," one of Boyd's favorite songs. Boyd was dressed—ironically, but again as he had requested—in the same black suit that he had worn at many funerals in recent years. Along with his wedding band, he was wearing his treble-clef, gold cufflinks and the twenty-fifth-anniversary ring that Harry had given him. The only other item in his casket was his trademark black trilby hat, which was not on his head but resting near his folded hands, as if he had removed it from his head just before taking a casual nap.

When Anita arrived to give her approval before the viewing, she fell to her knees beside the casket, weeping and clutching Boyd's once strong and warm, but now cold and lifeless, hands.

"My Boyd! My Boyd!" she sobbed, tears streaming down her cheeks.

As she regained her composure, she stood, wiping her face with a handkerchief, and told Boyd, "Now, Kevin's got something special planned for you. I know it. You'll see."

Anita was aware of Kevin's disease. Although she requested that some music be played softly during the wake, she asked that it be organized so that Kevin could participate with minimal disturbance. Selecting the music was not a problem: Dooley was familiar with Boyd's tastes and arranged a set of melancholy, soulful melodies—some jazz, some blues, and some ballads from the old-school rock 'n roll era. The music would be played only in a congregating room that was adjacent to the viewing room, allowing Kevin to be present and free from infection. Kevin planned to spend most of his time inside or near the viewing room, but also to occasionally make an appearance in the more social gathering room. In those cases, Barry or Dooley would simply turn off the music.

There was a remarkably upbeat, positive vibe to the wake. People spoke about what a joy it was to have known Boyd, about his bottomless well of wisdom, and of course his renowned passion for music. Music and people. Strangely, however, few people outside of the funeral home staff seemed to be aware of Boyd's unusual method of listening to a deceased person's favorite music while preparing the body. Yet none of the mourners were surprised to hear this fact as it was revealed by Kevin and Dooley several times over the course of the evening.

Friends and relatives made the trip from Alabama to pay their final respects. Classmates from Boston University spoke of his wit and charm around the campus. Neighbors and relatives had stories that captured his character and sense of humor. What astounded Kevin the most, however, despite having expected it, was the endless train of musicians from all walks of life: professionals, choir members, teachers, amateurs, and former fellow band members from his trumpet-playing days.

Many people were understandably saddened and distraught, especially when told of the unexpectedness of his death, but there always seemed to be two or three or more people in the vicinity who immediately recognized the sorrow and offered some uplifting thoughts:

"It was a great blessing to have known him."

"He enjoyed every breath he took."

"He's playing trumpet among the angels now."

Perhaps the most powerful condolence that Kevin heard was spoken by one of Boyd's neighbors: a longtime friend also in his late seventies. The man was trying to console Boyd's fourteen-year-old grandniece, who was crippled with grief and struggling to deal with the loss.

"My dear," the man told her, "only Boyd the man is no longer with us. But he was a spiritual, soul-inspired person, you know, and his soul he always shared with you, with all of us. He lived life to enrich his soul, you know, and that meant being part of *your* life, *your* spirit too. And you know, that is something that no one could ever, ever take away from you, no matter what. Part of who *you* are is part of who *Boyd* was. *Is.* As we knew him, as we know him. You still have his soul with you. And you are part of *his* soul. Don't you forget that."

It was essentially true, Kevin thought. Regardless of what anyone thinks happens to your soul when you die, or even if you believe there is such a thing as a soul at all, the essence of who you are, as Boyd once said, comes down to "relationships: what you've put into them, what you get out of them. That's it. The nature of your relationships determines what you get out of life, what everything means to you."

From Kevin's experience, these services often seemed to reflect the personality of those who were being remembered. This was the case with Boyd's: it was an atmosphere of pleasant exchanges, understanding, resilience, and humor.

*   *   *

The tone carried over into the funeral the next day. A traditional New Orleans funeral typically includes a musical procession led by a band from the church to the cemetery, or sometimes from the funeral home to the church. The processions, Kevin recalled from Boyd's descriptions, would be characterized by somber music played by an arrangement of jazz instruments. Boyd once explained that after everyone says their final goodbyes, the band "cuts the body loose" to a more upbeat tune such as "When the Saints Go Marching In," along the tempo similar to a Louis Armstrong rendition of the hymn.

However, Boyd insisted repeatedly that he never cared for the sadness of these processions or the despair of many funerals in general. Understanding this, Kevin had requested that the musicians prepare a livelier version of "Nearer My God to Thee" by Sarah Flower Adams and the classic gospel "Just a Closer Walk with Thee" for the procession itself. He assembled a group using the list that Boyd had provided: it included a snare drum, bass drum, trumpet, clarinet, trombone, tuba, tambourine, and choir singers. In addition, inside the church there would be a piano as well as an organ.

The McCormick Funeral Home was over two miles from Boyd's church, which would render a marching funeral procession difficult on a brisk, windy October day. The cemetery, on the other hand, was almost directly across the street from the church, making it very practical to execute the march.

During the funeral mass, for once Kevin managed to survive without any missing earplug incidents or misinterpretations from reading lips. The mourners sang along with the choir to a powerful, up-tempo version of John Newton's "Amazing Grace" and later to a similarly charged rendition of "I Saw The Light" by Hank Williams. Recalling how much Boyd encouraged Kevin to embrace the music and not fight his Musica Chorea, Kevin did not try to hide any movements that his body made due to the disease. Although the earplugs didn't entirely block out the sounds and vibrations from the music, they muffled the sounds enough that Kevin could maintain control.

The preacher's sermon was emotionally penetrating and effective, the theme of which was how "Brother Boyd devoted his life to preparing us for our journey to Jesus" and that "it was not merely through his profession, but through his way of life." He praised Boyd's character, describing it as the perfect blend of charisma and humility. He concluded that "We can be assured that our brother is completing his journey today."

Toward the latter half of the church service, there were four brief letters written to Boyd that were read by a few family members. They contained some stories and thanked him for his example and guidance.

Then the preacher called Kevin to the podium.

Kevin had never delivered a eulogy, although he had seen it done hundreds of times. He was apprehensive about his own emotion and its impact on his public speaking ability. Boyd had delivered Harry's eulogy, with a smoothness that Kevin admired and was certain he could not achieve with his own style. Nevertheless, whatever nerves Kevin felt disappeared as, at the moment the preacher called him, the reality of Boyd's death—and of his role in honoring Boyd's life – cemented his resolve. He took his place at the podium, acknowledging the crowd, Anita, the preacher, Boyd's family, his co-workers. He glanced toward Amy, who was seated beside Dotty, and gave them a quick, smiling nod.

"Boyd Oakley," he began, "was one of the rarest of gems to grace this world. We all know it. We all felt it. We feel it among us today. His entire life was about making connections to people: meaningful connections. He had a unique talent for people."

Kevin spoke briefly about Boyd's background: how he grew up in Alabama during a tumultuous period and came to Boston, where he met Anita. He explained how Boyd thought their relationship was doomed from the start because Anita didn't like the trumpet.

He recalled Harry's famous story about when Boyd was first interviewed at the McCormick Home, where Boyd nervously offered that "nobody took more pleasure in dealing with corpses than I, Mr. McCormick."

He spoke of Boyd's unparalleled knowledge of the history of music. He described the life that Boyd breathed into his work, and into the workplace in general.

"Boyd Oakley was not just a great mentor to us at work, but also in our personal lives. I don't believe he made any distinction between the two."

Then Kevin paused, fighting a lump that was forming in his throat, before he concluded by recalling a conversation he had had with Boyd recently, one that Kevin felt encapsulated Boyd's philosophy about life:

"Back when I was a naïve young man," he continued, "just a few weeks ago, struggling with some petty problem of mine, Boyd asked me a serious question. He said, 'What is your song going to be, Kevin?'

"I had no idea what he was talking about, so I replied, 'Something about pizza and beer. Or maybe the Outback Steakhouse jingle.'"

The crowd laughed and he heard someone shout 'Amen!'

"But he was trying to teach me something, as he so often did.

"So he asked me again, sternly, 'Seriously Kevin, I'm asking you.' He told me to 'Realize the perspective; that's what this amounts to. We all have a finite space here: a beginning and an end, an introduction and a finale. Filled with crescendos and dimuendos. Sometimes it's at adagio. Sometimes allegro.

"'Will it be capriccio? Will it have a chorus, or an interlude? A progression? Will it include a duet? Will it be sung by Pavarotti...Frankie Valli...Bruce Springsteen...or will it be sung by Alvin the Chipmunk?

"'And most importantly, Kevin, how will people feel when they hear it?'"

Kevin paused before repeating Boyd's question, this time steadily addressing the congregation, "What...is *your song*?"

He took a deep breath to settle his emotions, then concluded, "Thank you for your beautiful, humorous, charming, and inspiring song, Boyd. We love you. We love your song. We will all be sure to replay parts of it in our heads and hearts, over and over again."

*　　*　　*

Kevin removed the earplugs for the musical procession from the church to Boyd's final resting place in the nearby cemetery. Boyd's casket was carried by a single-horse-drawn hearse, followed by the musicians. The first song was a rhythm-and-blues version of Adams'

"Nearer My God to Thee," with a lively drumbeat. A soloist would sing part of the verse, leaving it to be completed by the rest of the choir. The brass and wind instruments provided wonderful proud puffs of filler between verses.

Behind the group of musicians formed the "second line," which was led by Kevin, Anita and Boyd's family members. In honor of Boyd, Kevin had decided to embrace his disease and to surrender his body completely to the music. To the upbeat R&B music, his body strutted, his shoulders jerking one at a time, his knees lifting to the beat, causing him to hop and spin. Whenever he began to steer off course, one of the family members or Amy was there to direct him back into the flow of the dancing, singing parade.

Police had blocked traffic so that the procession could march down the street from the church and then cross it to the cemetery. Some onlookers had gotten out of their cars to get a better look at the parade. Kevin had never heard of such a funeral in Malden, let alone near Boston itself. Some people had actually parked their cars to follow the parade.

The second song was the popular funeral hymn "Just a Closer Walk with Thee," played by the band with a similar lively style, except that the lead singer this time was a heavyset man who sang with a louder, more blues-filled, boisterous tone. The second line clapped and sang "Amen! Hallelujah, Amen!" between verses along with the instrumental accompaniment.

Boyd's burial plot was angled so that headstone faced the sunrise; fitting, Kevin thought, given how much Boyd had enjoyed sunrises. It was adjacent to a wooded area, as he had selected himself, so that not only he but also people visiting his grave would have the company of the birds that inhabited the woods year-round.

Before Boyd's casket was lowered into the grave, each mourner took a turn to either kiss the casket it, tap it, place a flower on it, or all of the above. As it was lowered into the grave, the band broke into a wild, jovial version of "When the Saints Go Marching In," heavily laden with fast-paced notes from the brass horns, cutting Boyd loose to the heavens.

The final song was an instrumental-only version of John Rosamond Johnson's "Didn't He Ramble." The band's rendition was a progression of solos from each brass and wind instrumentalist accompanied by the drums and tambourine, the first few notes introduced by the tuba, leading into the trombone, transitioning into the clarinet, which was finally overpowered by the trumpet. As the band played, some of the mourners took turns tossing shovelfuls of dirt over Boyd's grave, then dispersing as individuals or small groups. As the song wound to its end, Anita left accompanied by Boyd's siblings. Amy left with Dotty and Missy. The band also eventually dispersed, leaving only Kevin, Dooley, and Barry.

The three men stood over the half-buried casket of their friend and mentor. The only sounds were of an occasional chirp from one of the birds in the nearby trees.

"Hey," Barry finally said, breaking the silence, "We'd better return that horse before it makes a mess in the street. I don't want to clean that up."

"Yeah," Dooley agreed, "Me either. Good idea."

TWENTY

About a week after Boyd's funeral, Anita Oakley appeared at the funeral home to retrieve Boyd's personal items. When she was finished, she stopped by Kevin's office with one of her nephews, who carried a larger plastic storage container. She thanked Kevin for helping her "move mountains" for the company that handled Boyd's life insurance policy; the firm had required her to provide an unnecessary, excessive amount of documentation.

"Don't be a stranger," she told Kevin and gave him an embrace and a friendly kiss on the cheek.

"Oh, wait a minute," she stopped herself, "There was one other thing. I brought this in here with me, to give to you."

From her coat pocket, she retrieved a small box—the same small box that Boyd had presented to him months ago when Kevin fired him. Kevin had forgotten about the box, Boyd never mentioning it again.

"Oh, yes," Kevin noted, "I've seen this once before."

"Oh, I think you've seen it plenty of times."

"The box? No, I've only seen this box once. Boyd told me he wanted me to have it when we went our separate ways."

She handed it to him. The brown box was small enough to fit into his palm. Embroidered on the top was a single "B." Kevin flipped open the latch that held the top shut. He opened the lid.

Nestled in a small cushion inside the box was Boyd's gold twenty-fifth-anniversary ring, the diamonds of its musical design sparkling in the light.

"Mmmm-hmmm," Anita noted, seeing that the gesture had moved Kevin.

"Anita, this is…"

"That belongs here, Kevin. You take care of it."

"I will."

"Don't be a stranger now."

He hugged her again and led them out of the home.

*   *   *

After she left, Kevin took the box to the embalming room, to check on Dooley's progress with a recent round of clients. Dooley was in his surgical mask, gloves, with an apron draped around almost his entire body. He pulled down his mask as he noticed Kevin enter the room. A recently hired assistant was helping Dooley prepare the bodies. The room was eerily silent except for the tools and machines: a far cry from the sound of Boyd's music.

"How is she holding up?" Dooley asked, concerned about Anita.

"She's a strong woman," Kevin replied. "Dooley, I've got something here I think you should have."

"What's that?"

Kevin handed him the box. Dooley recognized the ring as soon as he flipped open the cover.

"Wow, geez Kev, I can't take this."

"Yes, you can," Kevin insisted, "I think it's better off in your hands. You deserve it."

The ring was about Boyd's process, Kevin believed, and nobody was closer to that than Dooley. Boyd had bonded with Dooley about music, even before Dooley began working for the home. Boyd was the one who had convinced Harry to give Dooley a shot and then took him under his wing, honing his skills, preparing him for the day when Dooley would take the reins. Dooley, in turn, embraced Boyd and his most essential tool: music. It was Dooley, Kevin decided, who understood and deserved the ring more than anyone else.

Dooley shook his head in disbelief. "Thank you, Kevin. I mean it. This is an incredible honor. I am not worthy of this."

"Yeah, but you are. It belongs with you."

He turned to leave the room. The quiet bothered him. As he walked towards the door, he recalled the many times he had entered that room with a list of music for Boyd. For all these years, he had dreaded asking that question of clients, but now he realized he was going to miss asking it.

"Wait, Kevin," Dooley called as Kevin approached the doorway.

"What?"

"You forgot something."

"I did? What's that?"

"The question. We don't have the list of music. You forgot to ask the question."

For sure, Kevin thought, turning to smile at Dooley, the ring is in the right hands. For sure.

With a nod, Dooley returned the expression, acknowledging the cumulative experience that gave Kevin's reflective grin meaning.

It was a smile that connected two souls.

"I'll get right on that," Kevin assured him, "We *will* have music."